YULE BE MINE

The Welwyn Marriage Wager
Book 3

By
Jenna Jaxon

ARE YOU SIGNED UP FOR DRAGONBLADE'S BLOG?

You'll get the latest news and information on exclusive giveaways, exclusive excerpts, coming releases, sales, free books, cover reveals and more.

Check out our complete list of authors, too!

No spam, no junk. That's a promise!

Sign Up Here

www.dragonbladepublishing.com

Dearest Reader;

Thank you for your support of a small press. At Dragonblade Publishing, we strive to bring you the highest quality Historical Romance from some of the best authors in the business. Without your support, there is no 'us', so we sincerely hope you adore these stories and find some new favorite authors along the way.

Happy Reading!

CEO, Dragonblade Publishing

Additional Dragonblade books by Author Jenna Jaxon

The Welwyn Marriage Wager Series
Until I'm Safe in Your Arms (Book 1)
The Baron's Halo (Book 2)
Yule Be Mine (Book 3)

The Lyon's Den Series
Pride of Lyons

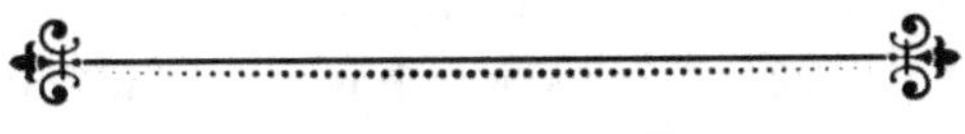

CHAPTER ONE

London, December 1, 1860

DESPITE LOSING AN obscene amount of money this morning, Ulysses Quartermain, Yule to friends and family, was having the time of his life. Standing in a corner in his grandfather's ballroom with his five cousins, celebrating his oldest cousin, Alex Bancroft's victory in the boxing ring, Yule couldn't imagine life being better. Well, not unless he had an inkling about which young lady he wanted to marry.

"Now we have two weddings down, who are we to wager on as being the next victim...er bridegroom?" Tom Weston, Yule's youngest cousin involved in the marriage wager, looked around the circle of gentlemen brightly. "Don't look at me, however. You can put me down in the book as being the last one to marry, Julius."

Julius, Lord Boxtd, duly produced the family's black, leather-bound wagers book and noted Tom's request. "Any takers on that, gentlemen?"

"I'll take some of that action, Julius." Francis, Julius's twin brother spoke up. "I plan to be the very last of us married. Tom will be an old married man by the time I tie the knot."

"You'd all better take note of the time you have left." Grandfather, the cause of all this marrying frenzy, took a long drink of something that looked a bit stronger than the champagne they were all drinking. "Alex and Sandy have done their duty handily. I salute you both." He raised his glass to the first two of the six cousins to marry. As one, they all raised their glasses accordingly and drank to the two surprisingly happy men. Surprising, because neither one had had a long courtship with the ladies they had married.

Yule drank willingly to his cousins' happiness, but secretly wondered how successful he would be in finding a lady he could love in the relatively short time allotted them to marry. Their grandfather had informed them in August that he'd been advised by his physician that he had only a year to live. To ease his mind that his eldest grandsons would do their family duty and marry, he'd proposed a wager that all six of them couldn't marry within the year. The prize, should they do so, was an estate for each, ten thousand pounds, and a carriage with its equipage. The catch was that all six had to enter the wager and all had to marry within the time frame or none received the prize.

Most of them had readily agreed to the terms, not unexpected as all Quartermain males had a fondness for wagers that bordered on the obsessed. Only two of them—Francis and Tom—had needed some persuasion. Those two were now racing to be the last to wed. Yule might actually give them a run for their money if he couldn't find the perfect woman to wed. The trouble was, he had no idea what he wanted in a wife.

"So are you going to be the next to fall, Yule?" Julius came over, drink in hand.

"I have serious doubts about it." Yule peered into this glass of champagne, the bubbles rising furiously from the bottom of the glass to the top.

"About marrying?" Julius's question was rather sharp. "Don't tell me you're going to be the first to renege on the wager? I'd have said Tom or Francis for sure, but never you."

"Why not me? There is no particular young lady I'm interested in at the moment." He cocked his head at his cousin. "I'd have thought you'd be the next one to say, 'I will.' You seemed awfully keen on Lady Augusta earlier this year. I heard rumblings about your match from my father even before Grandfather brought up the wager."

Julius scowled and downed his champagne in a single gulp. "If I'd had my way, I'd have been married last spring, or at the very least, the first one of us to wed for the wager." The man truly looked wretched. "I've wanted nothing but to marry Lady Augusta since we met last April. But she'll have none of it. No matter what I say, or what I do, she simply isn't interested."

"Do you know why? I'd think given your family connections—a duke for a grandfather on your mother's side and a title in your own right—Lady Augusta would be elated to accept you." Yule peered at his cousin who, granted, was very reticent unless in the bosom of the family. "You did actually ask the lady, didn't you, Julius?"

"Yes, I asked her." Julius's patience seemed to be wearing thin. "I've asked her, I've asked her father. I'd ask her butler if I thought that would do any good. I've done everything except have someone else woo her for me. She still says no."

"Did you tell her about the marriage wager? Is that what put her off you?" Their newly married cousin Alex had insisted they all tell any prospective bride about the wager right away, so there'd be no issue arising from it.

"She knows, although I didn't tell her. But she refused me even before we made the wager with Grandfather."

"Does she say why, then?"

"She's not in love with me." The exasperated sigh from his cousin was obviously heartfelt.

"And that's her only impediment?"

"It's enough to make her say no each of the five times I've asked her to marry me." Julius's expression was the perfect blend of anger and misery.

"You have my sympathies, although my problem is quite the opposite. I have no attachment to any lady at the moment. I truly envy you and Alex and Sandy. You at least know what you want, and the two of them managed to find the perfect women with little effort indeed." Yule knew himself better than to think he would be able to do that so easily. "It's not as though I'm terribly fastidious about it. A pretty woman is always a plus, but I'm not set on finding a beauty. And my finances are such I don't need to marry an heiress, thank goodness. Still I'm having the devil of a time finding someone who appeals to me. Now that most of the *ton* is going back home for the winter months, I likely won't meet anyone new or be able to develop an interest in another lady until the spring. Then I'm going to be as rushed as Tom and Francis to find a bride."

"Well, I wish you luck, cousin. Are you heading back to the estate in Hertfordshire for Christmas or staying in Town with Grandfather?"

"Mother and Father want to be here to be close to Grandfather. Just as well, I suppose. More people to meet in London than out in the frozen countryside." Yule shrugged. He didn't hold out much hope of finding a bride in either place.

"Are you planning to come to Herr Kastner's Christmas party next week?"

"Fritz Kastner? From Oxford?" That was a name Yule hadn't heard in years.

"The very one. His father is having a Christmas party to celebrate one of the Kastner sisters' betrothal. Mother received an invitation a few days ago." Julius looked eager for the first time that evening. "I've been assured Augusta will be there."

"Don't you think you should perhaps pay attention to some other young lady, Julius? Whatever you've been doing isn't getting the desired effect. Perhaps if you show her you've moved on, she might become jealous. Begin to pursue you for a change."

"That would be quite nice." Julius didn't look convinced.

"Why don't we set ourselves a little wager regarding the party, then?" Yule grinned, hoping to encourage Julius to move forward with his courting. "The first one of us to secure an invitation to tea with a new young lady wins the bet. How does that sound? Something to give us an incentive to mingle at the party."

"When you say new, do you mean someone we've not met before?" Julius dug the wager book out of his jacket pocket. "Or simply a young lady we've not previously shown an interest in?"

Yule thought for a moment. What were the chances of unknown ladies turning up at the Kastner party? Well, some of their unknown relatives from Germany perhaps, but otherwise that was doubtful. "The latter I think. It's so difficult to meet completely new ladies this time of year."

"Agreed." Julius wrote the wager down in his meticulous script. "You've really had no luck at all finding someone you think will suit you?"

"I did have hopes for a brief time of Lady Cora Hastings. We'd been introduced at some garden party last year, before she was out. Then I met her again this past August at Lord Caxton's house party where Alex met Emma. We seemed to suit rather well, I thought. She and I share an interest in Greek mythology— we had a very spirited discussion of my namesake and his journey home one evening—and while that can't be considered a major reason to marry someone, shared interests certainly help."

"But you don't think Lady Cora is interested in pursuing a courtship with you?" Julius looked sympathetic.

"No, not a chance. I heard last week she's become betrothed to Lord Roydon." Yule shrugged. "It's no matter. My heart was not engaged in the slightest." But he thought it could have been, had there been more time to spend with the lady. After the house party, however, her family had headed north to Scotland for grouse hunting. Yule had let the matter slip his mind what with Alex's wedding and then the debacle of Sandy being jilted at the altar. He'd had his own affairs to see to as well, and then last week his mother had mentioned Lady Cora's betrothal.

"Buck up, old chap." Julius' face lit up with an uncharacteristic grin. "You're now pitted against me to find a bride. Given my history, your luck's bound to change for the better."

Yule laughed and slapped his cousin on the back. There was nothing like family to raise one's spirits.

December 6
Ashford, Kent, England

THE DRAWING ROOM at Ashland Park had been furnished with understated splendor to Yule's eye as he and Fritz Kastner reminisced about their university days at Oxford. The sage green walls, with their elegant white and gold molding, exuded calm. The furniture complimented both the color and the style of the room, several chaise lounges, a camelback sofa, and numerous chairs were scattered around the room in clever groupings that invited guests to sit and sip the beverage of their choice. Yule and his friend had opted for the somewhat stronger brandy, and now stood near the bowed window that looked out over the stunning parkland belonging to the estate.

A restful house, to be sure. Yule could easily see himself settling down in one like this, with the proper wife to run it for him, that was. Keeping an ear on the conversation, Yule kept an eye cocked in anticipation of finding a young lady who would help him win his wager with Julius by inviting him to tea, and perhaps winning his heart as well. At least, Yule still lived in hopes something of the sort would happen. Not so much for the wager's sake, for once, but for his own happiness.

He returned his attention to his friend. "I understand your sister Elise is to be married in the New Year. I shall give her my felicitations as soon as I see her." Yule breathed deeply, then ventured a question. "You have three sisters, as I recall, Fritz. Are the others married as well?"

"Yes, Elise was the baby of the family," his friend said, smiling broadly. "Anna married the year I graduated from university, and

Suzanna followed the year after." Fritz grinned. "I am now the only one of us still unfettered, and likely to remain so for some time. I have a business to run and a house to acquire before I can think of marriage." Fritz cocked his head. "You are also too young to think of marriage, are you not, Ulysses?"

"Well…" Yule didn't want to dissemble, exactly, but neither did he wish the marriage wager to be broadcast during the weekend. "A gentleman of my station is always watching out for the right young lady, should she come along."

"Ah, yes, the English drive to marry and father an heir early in your life." His friend shook his head. "That is fine for the ladies, I suppose. But we gentlemen need to 'sow our wild oats' as they say, do we not?"

"My cousin Tom Weston certainly seems to think so." Yule shook his head. Ever since Grandfather had given him his ship, Tom had become one of the *ton's* worst rakes. Rumors, as well as eye-witness accounts, of his carousing and taking up with a stream of mistresses had come to the ears of the family. Grandfather had simply laughed and made a bet as to how many women Tom would bed before he settled down and married. "He's made it clear he's not got marriage on his mind yet."

"Perhaps we three shall make a pact not to marry until we are at least thirty." Fritz laughed and snagged a glass from a passing footman.

"With your determination, Tom and I would be at quite a disadvantage." For other reasons as well, of course.

"I'm sorry, Ulysses. We have additional guests arriving, I see." Fritz set his drink down. "Please allow me to excuse myself. I've been pressed into service to help as host tonight by my parents."

"Of course, old man. When duty calls." Yule waved him on, and his friend hurried to the doorway where a family had just entered. A father, mother, and two daughters…

Gazing at the young ladies, Yule's rational thoughts ceased. Both young ladies were beautiful, however the slightly smaller one, willowy and dressed in a lovely green flowy gown captured his attention first. The gown's bodice, cut in a deep vee, showed her figure to excellent advantage. A large emerald pendant nestled in at the top of her decolletage drew his gaze immediately, the emerald drop earrings keeping his attention fastened on the vivacious lady. Her deep auburn hair glittered in the flickering candlelight, making it seem like molten copper.

Yule's heart began to race, his cock coming to attention in an instant. Where had this entrancing creature been hiding? He certainly had never been introduced to her, so perhaps she wasn't out in Society yet. Still, that would mean she was almost of marriageable age.

And Fritz must know her and could introduce her to him.

Yule smiled his widest, about to start across the room to where his friend was speaking to the parents, when the young lady spied him, and her face broke into a broad smile that changed her from being simply beautiful to the most exquisite creature he'd ever beheld.

Amazingly, she started toward him. "Sissy? Is that you?"

Yule froze, the childish nickname dousing his ardor like a face full of snow. No one had ever called him that but—

"Sissy! Don't you recognize me?" She'd arrived at his side and to his chagrin, threw her arms around him. "It's me, P—"

"Penelope St. Claire." Good God. The little girl next door to his grandparents' estate in Hertfordshire, where he'd lived all his life. The last time he'd seen Penelope had been—Christ, had it been ten years? She'd been seven when her father had been appointed to a government post in Northern Ireland and the family had moved away.

"You remembered me." She hugged him tighter, making him cringe.

Somehow it seemed obscene for a little girl to be embracing him in a way that threatened to arouse him. This was absurd. Yule managed to put her from him. "Hello, Penelope. I hadn't been told your family had returned to London."

She peered up into his face, her smile fading. "We have just come to Town. Charlotte, my sister, and I are to have our come outs during the next Season. Papa wanted to get the family settled, now before Christmas, but the tenant renting the estate can't leave before the New Year. So we are fixed in London for Christmas." She gazed at him, yearning in her gaze. "Will you be here or at your grandfather's estate?"

Much as he'd love to say he'd be in Hertfordshire, it would do no good to lie. Penelope would discover the truth eventually. "We are in London. Grandfather came up for a sporting event last week and decided to remain through the New Year." More than anything, he wished to stalk off and leave her, but he could not be rude, not even to Penelope. "Your parents and sister are well?"

"Very well, thank you." She seemed to expect more, but he had no idea what to say to her. The last time he'd seen her, he'd given her a doll to take with her to Ireland. What did one say to a young lady who was hardly more than a child still?

"Are your parents well?"

Yule sighed. He couldn't stand here exchanging inane pleasantries with Penelope. "They are well also. I suspect both our parents will find one another and catch up after such a long time."

"You and I should catch up as well, Sissy." Her smile came back, more tentative this time. "It has been a long time since we last met. I was quite a little girl then."

"Yes, you were." Ten years had changed her, to be sure, still he couldn't stop thinking of her as the child he'd known then.

"I am quite grown up now." She raised her chin, her petite nose still dusted with freckles.

She must be at least seventeen now if she was going to have her Season in the spring. Yule shook his head. He could not get past the idea that this lovely creature was little Penelope, with the big blue eyes and carrot red hair that stuck out all over her head. "I can scarcely believe it."

Her expression hardened, as though his response was not what she'd been expecting. "Well, try harder then, Sissy. I am as old now as you were when you thought yourself grown up." Her eyes snapped with anger. "You'll just have to get used to the change." She grasped her skirts, turned on her heel with a flounce, and sped back across the room to rejoin her parents.

Yule watched her go, shaking his head in utter disbelief. Nothing could have prepared him for the fact that the most desirable woman he'd ever seen had turned out to be the little girl next door.

CHAPTER TWO

"READY FOR A nightcap?" Julius stood next to the sideboard, his glass of brandy topped almost to overflowing as Yule entered the Kastner's library. He had, in fact, been seeking a libation and supposed the library would be the least crowded place to find one.

"Absolutely." Weary after an evening of forcing pleasant conversation and avoiding Penelope St. Claire, he needed a whole bloody decanter to himself.

"You sound as discouraged as I feel." His cousin topped off another glass and handed it to Yule before taking a large gulp from his own. "I swear there are no unattached ladies of any sort at this house party, save the St. Claire daughters and they are a trifle young for my tastes."

"They are indeed." The excellent cognac slid down Yule's throat with a pleasant burn, exploding in his stomach, then mellowing, and easing the strange apprehension he'd been suffering from all evening. "Strange, I didn't recognize her at first, but then, it's been ten years since the family left Hertfordshire. Changes in appearance were bound to happen."

"Which one?" Julius looked at him oddly.

"Which one what?" Yule took another gulp of the life restoring cognac.

"You said you didn't recognize *her*. To which Miss St. Claire are you referring?"

"Not *Miss* St. Claire. Penelope, of course. The little one with red hair and freckles." Why that image of her disturbed him so much, he didn't understand at all. "She and her brother Victor used to come over to play with me quite often. Victor and I played together, that is. Penelope sort of tagged along. Her sister was friends with my sisters, Iphigenia in particular, as I recall." Yule shook his head. "Damned shame when Victor died." He took another sip of the brandy. His friend had contracted scarlet fever at the age of fifteen and died shortly afterward. "Not long after that, the family left for Ireland."

"So, you knew them all well." Julius had taken a seat in a comfortable-looking leather chair.

"Yes, I did. Although I was closer to Penelope and Victor." Yule continued to stand by the sideboard. He might need more than one drink before bed. "She was a funny little thing, always trying to do whatever we boys were doing, but dragging along this beastly, ragged doll everywhere with her."

"Little girls are prone to do that, I believe. At least my sisters did." Julius eyed him strangely over his brandy.

"Mine were some years older than I, so I didn't pay much attention to what they did." Suddenly cursed with too much energy, Yule began to pace about the library recalling the last time he'd seen Penelope before tonight. "They left almost at dawn one morning, in early autumn. The leaves were falling everywhere, flame-colored like Penelope's hair. I hadn't seen her in a few months, not since Victor's death. She'd caught the disease too, but somehow had survived. But they all came by Grandfather's on their way to the train to say goodbye."

Funny how he could recall that morning so well, as though it had happened just last week. "Everyone was taking their leave, still in mourning, so it was very solemn. And they were pretty much ignoring Penelope, who was only seven. I'd missed Victor all those weeks, missed Penelope too. I'd sent notes to her mother asking after her. I'd been horrified when they told me they'd had to cut her hair off because of the fever. And they'd taken her little rag doll from her as well, afraid it had caused the disease. I hated that and felt so sorry for Penelope. So, I'd asked Mother to get me a doll to give her. I told Penelope she might not have many friends when she first got to Ireland, so I was giving her a friend to take with her, to replace the one she'd lost."

"You must have become her hero on the spot." Julius smiled.

"I suppose I did." Yule turned to stare out the window.

Penelope's big blue eyes, still sunk back in her head from the illness, had widened like saucers when he'd bent down and handed her the doll with a painted porcelain face, dressed in an elegant blue gown. Gingerly, she'd taken it, then thrown her arms around him saying, "Oh, thank you, Sissy. I'll love her always." Then she'd stepped back and gazed up at him. "What's her name?"

"Mrs. Phillpotts. She is a very wise, very friendly lady. She's someone you can talk to when there's no one else to listen to you." Why he'd told her that he had no idea, just that he'd understood Penelope must be feeling bad and missing Victor even more than he did. If the doll could make up for that loss even a little, he'd be delighted.

"And now she's all grown up." Julius finished his cognac and set the glass on the table beside him.

"She's hardly that." Yule took another long sip and turned back to Julius. "I can scarcely believe she's having a Season in the spring, although I suppose she'll be eighteen in February." Could she really be that old? Well, he'd be twenty-eight this coming summer, so yes, it was possible.

"She was certainly acting grown up this evening." Julius eyed the decanter, as if considering pouring another drink. "I saw her talking quite animatedly with Lord Clavering later in the evening." His cousin gave Yule a sidelong look. "One might even call it flirting."

"Who is Lord Clavering?" The words came out sharper than Yule had intended.

"He inherited the viscountcy from an uncle in Essex, about six months ago. He's just out of mourning and very keen on doing his duty by the title." Julius grinned. "Young puppy, but he'll settle down."

"How does Fritz know him?" Yule had been too busy trying to avoid Penelope to notice Clavering, but that didn't mean he wasn't interested in the man's antecedents.

"The late uncle was a friend of the family."

"Well, if he's young, perhaps he would suit Penelope." Yule stared into the dregs of his cognac. Funny to be talking so much about her this evening, when he'd never thought about the girl even once after he'd seen her off to Ireland that morning.

Of course, he'd gone to university that autumn, and on his Grand Tour four years later. Once he'd returned to England, he'd settled into his digs in London, happy to live the life of a gentleman with very few cares in the world—until Grandfather had set them the marriage wager. Now he'd actually have to find himself a wife—and pray he did better than he had tonight. Best stop thinking about Penelope St. Claire and focus his attention on finding an eligible young lady. "So did you get an invitation to tea, Julius?"

"No." His cousin spit out the word and rose, picked up his glass, and headed back to the sideboard. "I spoke to several young ladies, but they all turned out to be married or betrothed."

"This party isn't going to have as good hunting for us as I originally thought." Yule shook his head. Lord Caxton's house party in August had come to mind immediately, where he'd met at least three young ladies who were unattached. His cousin Alex had actually found his bride at that gathering, which proved such parties could end in matrimony. Just not at this party. "I received an invitation to tea, but it was from Lady St. Claire, so that hardly counts."

"It's closer than I've come." Julius had poured himself another drink and was staring morosely into the glass. "And Penelope and Miss St. Claire will likely be there as well, so I'm willing to concede the wager to you. No one wishes to speak to me for more than five minutes, much less invite me to tea for half an hour."

"Let's not be hasty, Julius." Yule held up his hand. "Tomorrow Fritz and his family are planning a trip into the woods to gather greenery and play Mistletoe Run. Perhaps they will invite some additional guests—some additional young ladies from the neighborhood—to come out in the woods with us."

"That's a long shot, Yule."

"Since when have you not been willing to try to beat the odds, Julius?"

His cousin sighed and drained his glass. "As you say, cousin. I'll let it ride."

SITTING AT THE toilette table in the pretty little guest room she shared with her sister, brushing her hair before the mirror, Penelope frowned at her reflection. Tonight's meeting with Ulysses Quartermain had scarcely been the encounter she'd been dreaming about for years, and she wasn't exactly sure why. "Charlotte, can I ask you something?"

Her sister had just finished washing her face and stepped from behind the hand-painted screen with Japanese cherry blossoms on black lacquer. "What is it, Pen?"

"What can I do to make Sissy like me?" Penelope rushed through the question, although she'd been thinking about nothing else ever since her old friend had walked away after scarcely speaking two words to her after an absence of ten years.

"Well, the first thing you can do is to stop calling him 'Sissy.'" Her sister pulled back the covers and slid into the soft bed. "Really, Penelope, why would you think a grown man would want to be called such a silly nickname?" Charlotte began stuffing her blond hair up underneath her nightcap. "I don't blame him for not wanting to talk to you. You likely embarrassed him."

"But I thought he'd like to remember the fun times we had when we were young. Before Victor died." Penelope joined her sister in the bed, twisting her dark auburn locks into a knot on top of her head, then pulling the cap over it. "He didn't seem to mind me calling him that then."

"You were seven years old, Pen. He probably minded but didn't let on because you were a child. If you want him to talk to you like you are a young lady, you need to act like it. And start by calling him Ulysses." Charlotte lay back on the pillow and pulled the cover up to her chin. As if something had suddenly occurred to her, she flipped over toward Penelope and plucked at the sleeve of her nightgown. "Do you mean you want him to talk to you like a gentleman talks to a young lady he's interested in courting, or simply as a friend?"

Hesitating, Penelope quickly weighed her options. She'd done so much to make sure of this meeting with Sissy after all these years. She couldn't let the opportunity go by to learn whatever her sister might know about how to make a gentleman fall in love with you. "I want him to court me, Charlotte."

"Oh." Her sister flopped back down on the mattress. "I suppose I should have expected that. You've dragged that doll he gave you all over." She cut her gaze over at Penelope. "Is that why you wheedled Mama into asking Lord and Lady Hugh into getting us an invitation to this house party? I know our family doesn't know the Kastners at all."

Sheepishly, Penelope nodded. "I knew we were coming to London for Christmas, and I'd heard you say you'd had a letter from Yule's sister, Iphigenia, mentioning Yule would be in London after this house party." She shrugged. If she wanted something thing, she had to go after it. "I merely pointed out to Mama that it would be very jolly if we could meet the Quartermains here, because house parties inevitably have bachelors in attendance. And we are coming out in the spring. Why not get a head start on things?"

"Penelope!" Charlotte sat up in the bed. "You are incorrigible."

"Is that truly such a bad thing to be?" Penelope sat up beside her, her head cocked to the side. She knew what she wanted. Why shouldn't she go after it?

After giving her sister a long hard look, Charlotte heaved a sigh, and settled down under the covers again. "Oh, very well then. The first thing to do is call him by his proper name."

"You mean Ulysses? Not Yule? That's what the family calls him, you remember."

Charlotte propped her head up on her hand. "I'd start by calling him Ulysses and let him suggest Yule if he wants you to be that familiar. You never called him that before, so you'd better act more respectfully to begin with."

Sliding down under the covers too, Penelope nodded. "I'll try that when I see him tomorrow." Burning to know more about how Yule might address her if he wanted to court her, but wanting to include her sister in the conversation out of politeness, Penelope ventured a question. "Did you meet anyone you might be interested in tonight, Charlotte?"

Her sister lay back on her pillow, her brow furrowed. "There were actually several young men I could take a fancy to. Lord Boxtd, I seem to remember when he was a boy visiting Welwyn Manor in the summer. He was as wild as all the Quartermain cousins then, but he's rather more reserved now. His profile is quite handsome in a brooding sort of way. Then there's Mr. Kastner, who is also rather dark and dashing. I think I would like to get to know them better this weekend."

"What does a young lady do to get to know these gentlemen better?" Penelope bounded up in the bed, eager to find out what to do to get Ulysses to notice her at all.

"Well," Charlotte sat up, excitement brewing in her face, "tomorrow I understand after breakfast, we will all go out to the woods to cut greenery for the house, including a Christmas tree. I hope to be paired with either Lord Boxtd or Mr. Kastner and with luck, we will strike up some light conversation. You want to let the gentlemen know you have some wits about you as well as a sense of humor. A gentleman always wishes for his wife to be a good companion and be able to converse on a variety of topics. But most importantly, they want a wife who has sense and an organizational bent to her, so she will be able to run their households capably from the very first."

"Where did you learn all this, Charlotte? Mama never spoke of any of this to me." It was rather surprising and not at all fair her mother had entrusted all these wiles to her sister but not to her. Perhaps Charlotte had become her favorite while Penelope hadn't been watching. Or maybe it was just because Charlotte was older.

"Mama has told me nothing about the courting process, save to listen to gentlemen whenever they speak and don't gainsay them at all costs." Charlotte sat up, making a rude face. "If we had to wait for her to tell us how to catch a beau, we'd both be old maids. You know how she is."

"Oh, I certainly do. 'Mind your manners and run along, my dear, and don't bother me.'" Penelope frowned. "Then how did you—"

"Phaedra and Iphigenia Quartermain told me all this years ago. We've corresponded with one another over the years, as you know. Do you remember them at all?"

Penelope shook her head. "Only that they are Ulysses's twin sisters. I was always off with him and Victor."

"They were a few years older than I, but I was always sent off to sit with them whenever Mama called on their mother. Iphigenia took a liking to me for some reason, and we became good friends after a while. Being older, *she* knew quite a lot about young gentlemen. And one time, after their eldest sister, Cassandra had just been married, they told me all about how she'd instructed to catch a beau."

"Goodness! And you remember such things from all that long ago?" Rapt, Penelope drank in the Quartermain's intelligence as though it was ice cold water on a hot summer's day.

"Yes, they were so insistent that I should learn from Cassandra as well, I've never forgotten it." Charlotte leaned closer, seeming to warm to her subject. "And it's a good thing too, now we're both of marriageable age. Let me see. What else did they say? Oh, if a gentleman hovers around you, conversing for more than a few minutes, then he's interested in you."

"Will they be talking about anything in particular?" Making mental notes, Penelope prayed she'd remember all this in the morning.

"No, I don't think so. Subjects like the weather, the health of family and friends, deaths or marriages they have heard of, or people like Charles Dickens or the Queen, or the theatre—things like that are all fair game." Charlotte nodded sagely.

"So talking to you excessively is a sign of their regard." Her sister had just said that a prospective husband wished his wife to know about a variety of topics, so speaking about them with her would help him ascertain that. "Is there anything else a prospective suitor will do?"

"If he asks for more than one dance, you can be certain he is interested in you."

"Lord Clavering has asked for two dances with me at the ball tomorrow night." Penelope smiled, remembering the eagerness of the young lord. "I promised him one, but said I'd already promised the others. I thought that was prudent, don't you?" Yule, however, hadn't asked for a single dance. Well, she'd have to remedy that, wouldn't she?

"It may be, however you don't want to have to sit out a single dance, do you? Ladies have to exhibit their skill at dancing whenever possible. Gentlemen set a great store by how well a woman dances." Charlotte frowned. "Although I'm not quite sure I understand why. Once you are married, you are never allowed to dance with your husband in public again."

"Perhaps there are private dances married couples can attend." Penelope had no real idea, but that seemed a sensible possibility.

"Perhaps."

"Is there anything else?" She'd no idea her sister would be such a fount of courting knowledge.

"Yes, and you must pay close attention to this one, Pen." Charlotte stared straight at her, her mouth drawn into serious lines. "Iphigenia said it was most important."

"What?" Penelope leaned closer to her sister.

"If a gentleman asks you to walk in the garden during the day, that also means he is interested in pursuing you. However, if he asks you to go out into the garden at *night*—" Charlotte paused and drew the covers back up around her, "—he may be interested in…other things."

"What other things?" Penelope whispered, though she and Charlotte were quite alone.

"It means he wants to take liberties. Like kissing you." Eyes boring into Penelope, Charlotte's cheeks grew pink. "You do you know about kissing, don't you, Pen? And what it can lead to?"

Penelope nodded, thoughtful, even though she wasn't quite sure what kissing led to. Her mother had merely told her to be careful about letting gentlemen take advantage of her, although she hadn't elaborated on what that meant. She'd said it would be soon enough for Penelope to learn about such things just before her Season began. But Penelope had seen people kissing under the mistletoe for years, so she understood the basic mechanics of it. Now, however, she was going to be able to participate in it. "I heard Mr. Kastner say that after gathering the greenery, we are to play Mistletoe Run. There's kissing in that game, isn't there?"

"Yes, there is." Charlotte sighed. "I cannot wait to see who I'll be paired with. I can only hope it will be Lord Boxtd or Fritz Kastner." She shot Penelope a sly glance. "Or Mr. Weston. He's quite the most handsome gentleman in the party, don't you think?"

"Oh, indeed. He is quite the handsomest gentleman." Although perhaps not the most handsome one in her opinion. "Why haven't you set your cap for him?"

"I'm not setting my cap for anyone until the spring. Well…perhaps I might set it for Lord Boxtd." Her sister giggled. "There's just something about a brooding gentleman that makes me want to comfort him."

"Oooh, Charlotte." Penelope laughed. "Or should I say, Lady Boxtd?"

"No, say nothing of the sort, I beg you." Her sister whirled around and blew out the lamp, plunging them into darkness. "I'd be mortified if he should come to know of my particular regard."

"Your secret is safe with me, Charlotte. You have my promise." Penelope slid back down in the bed and pulled the covers up to her chin. "Good night."

"Good night." Charlotte turned over and in a few moments was breathing rhythmically, then slowly and deeply.

Penelope stared out into the darkness, thinking about what Charlotte had just told her. Tomorrow she would have a chance, perhaps, to make Ulysses see her as grown up. She would take her sister's advice and only address him by his given name. She'd speak to him about the approved topics to let him see how well she could act like a young lady. Surely then she could find a way to persuade him to ask her for a dance. And then, during the Mistletoe Run, if she was lucky, she could get him to kiss her.

Because once he kissed her, he'd have no doubt whatsoever that she was a *very* eligible young lady who was more than ready for him to court her.

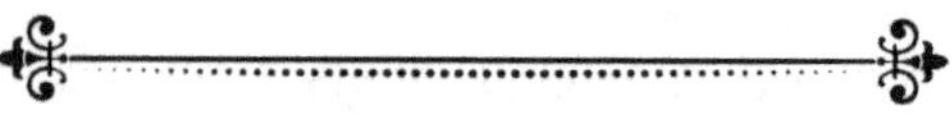

CHAPTER THREE

T HE MORNING HAD dawned crisp and cold, but then that was the usual way of it in December. Yule gazed out the drawing room window over the frozen lawn, the sun's thin rays tinging the snow with faint streaks of pink. For some reason, the hint of color made him think of Penelope's cheeks before she'd stalked back to her parents last night. Strange how his thoughts kept returning to the child. He supposed it might be because her appearance last night had been such a shock. He really needed to concentrate on what eligible ladies were available this weekend so he could at least attempt to think about getting on with the wager.

"Yule, good morning." Fritz clamped him on the shoulder. "I trust you slept well. Have you breakfasted yet?"

"I have. Always a bit of an early riser, if you remember." Yule smiled at his friend. "I might just nip back in for another cup of coffee."

"A good idea, as we are heading out into the woods in about half an hour. The plan is to collect the greenery and tree this morning, decorate the house this afternoon in preparation for the ball this evening." His friend grinned, then turned toward another gentleman who'd just entered the room. "Carrington, good morning. Can I get a word?" Fritz tapped Yule's shoulder. "Be sure to dress warmly."

"I will," Yule called as his friend hurried after the other guest. "Good morning, Ulysses."

Yule's head snapped back around, and he gasped.

Penelope stood before him, smiling radiantly, dressed in a very smartly cut walking gown in a bold blue and black plaid, trimmed in black that made her waist seem small enough for him to span with his hands. An elegant blue velvet bonnet accented in black hid much of her red hair but made her eyes a dazzling sapphire. For a moment, it was again as though he didn't know who she was, just like last night when he first saw her across the room.

He returned her smile. "Good morning, Penelope. You are looking well this morning." Better than well, to be sure. She looked most attractive.

"As do you. I understand we are going to gather greenery this morning. The weather is fortunately clear, though it looks terribly cold." She nodded to the icy scene outside the window.

"I daresay we will be chilly at first, but our efforts may warm us up sufficiently." He hoped her mother would make sure Penelope dressed warmly enough.

"Yes, the Mistletoe Run should take care of that quite nicely." Her eyes sparkled as she spoke the words, making Yule's stomach drop.

It would be damned awkward if he was paired with Penelope for that kissing game. He'd have to make certain he was partnered with some other young lady.

"Do you think we might fetch the greenery together, Ulysses? I'd like to catch up, see what you've been up to all this time." Her low-pitched, lyrical voice was lovely to listen to.

There was no reason why they couldn't do the gathering together. Nothing at all strange about that. They hadn't seen one another in such a long time, of course Penelope would be curious about what he'd been doing. He'd likely do most of the talking, of course. Not much for her to tell about her life in Ireland. Still, it would be good to find out how she'd fared in a strange land, without her brother. "That sounds like a splendid idea, Penelope."

Her face lit up, just as it had when he'd given her that doll, Mrs. Phillpotts, he recalled. A beautiful face, to be sure, but so young. He'd simply have to make damned sure he had a different partner for the mistletoe game.

"Have you been reading Mr. Dickens's most recent novel?" The eagerness in her voice made him smile. "It's called *Great Expectations*, serialized in his magazine *All the Year Round*. I think it's quite a good story so far. The third installment comes out today."

"I have not begun that one, although I have read quite a few of Mr. Dickens's novels." He was rather a fan of the author's works. "When did it begin?"

"Just two weeks ago, on December first."

"Ah, well, no wonder I didn't read it. There was quite a to-do at my grandfather's house that weekend." Lord, that had been an eventful two days.

"Do tell, Ulysses." She stepped closer, her eyes eager. "You always told such good stories when you were a boy."

"Parts of this one will curl your hair. Are you certain you can stand such a tale?" Her parents had likely already had it from his parents, so he wouldn't be telling anything out of turn.

She raised her chin. "Try me."

Yule glanced around to find the guests filing out of the room. They must be heading for the waggonettes that would take them to the woods. "Come, we mustn't miss our carriage. I'll tell you on the way out."

Nodding, she started toward the doorway.

"Oh, Penelope."

She halted and glanced at him over her shoulder. "Yes?"

"Please call me Yule. Everyone else does." Only strangers called him Ulysses so it sounded odd coming from little Penelope. Better than the dreadful "Sissy" of course, but too formal for her. He offered her his arm.

"Thank you, Yule." She took his arm, her touch strangely warm, and they proceeded to the foyer to don coats against the chill of the day.

Yule tugged at his collar. If he continued to feel this heated, he might not need his overcoat at all.

TRUE TO HIS word, Yule told Penelope all about the boxing match between his cousin Alexander and Alex's uncle that had occurred on December first and how it, and all the other wagers riding on the outcome, had turned out well for some of his cousins, although not for him. By the time he'd finished that tale, they had arrived at their destination deep in the Kasters's woods. Therefore, he refrained from informing her of the nasty turn of events that had transpired on the following day, involving his cousin Sandy and his new wife Isabelle. Just as well keep that story for another day.

"My father always said the Quatermains would take any wager, no matter how trivial or strange," Penelope laughed as Yule helped her down from the waggonette.

"He was certainly correct in that. It seems to be a trait handed down through the years, for my father has made his share of wagers, and Grandfather is possibly the worst of all." It was on the tip of his tongue to tell her about the marriage wager, but Fritz was calling them all to gather at a part of the clearing, so Yule again offered his arm and they joined the rest of the guests, their breaths visible in the frosty air.

"My family's gratitude to everyone for helping us celebrate the holiday this year," Fritz announced to the crowd and a good-natured murmur sprang up all over the clearing. "If everyone would go into the woods and gather as much greenery as you possibly can—this includes holly, ivy, bayberry, rosemary, and of course, mistletoe—we would be very appreciative. We have brought baskets just for this purpose. The footmen are distributing them to everyone. The best way to get as much greenery as possible we have found, is for everyone to break into teams of two or three and head into the woods in all different directions. We will meet back here in approximately one hour, at which time we will serve wassail and have a game of Mistletoe Run. My father and I will locate a suitable mistletoe ball, clear the space beneath it, and let the game begin. Good luck to you all."

"Which way should we go, Yule?" Penelope snagged a long-handled basket from a passing footman and turned to him, her face bright and eager.

"Let's head out this way." Yule pointed toward a stand of oak trees to the west of the clearing. "That way the sun will be at our backs, not in our faces."

"That suits me." Before he could offer his arm, Penelope headed into the woods in the direction he'd pointed.

Yule followed after her, intrigued by the change in her from last night. She'd gone from calling him Sissy and not knowing what to say to being a calm, thoughtful young woman who'd used his proper name for possibly the first time in her life. What had come over her? Had her mother noticed their interaction last night and talked some sense into her? He wasn't sure, but he was definitely grateful for the alteration. He hurried his pace until he overtook her and offered his arm. The day had shifted from being a burden he'd prefer to avoid, to a fun outing with an interesting companion. "So you are enjoying the new Dickens novel? Tell me about it so you can catch me up. The next installment becomes available today, you said?"

Smiling broadly up into his face, Penelope launched into the saga of Pip Pirrip and his unfortunate Christmas. The snow crunched companionably under their boots as Penelope talked and they began to find the proper sprigs of greenery.

They came upon a patch of holly bushes and Yule took out a pocketknife and began to cut large branches from the prickly shrubs. The cuttings were dropped carefully into the large basket, then they moved on toward a rosemary bush. In a remarkably short amount of time, the basket was brimming full of fragrant holly, rosemary, and bayberry branches.

"The scents are heavenly." Penelope stuck her nose close to the heap of cuttings. "Nothing makes me think of Christmas more than the smell of bayberry."

"For me, it's the smell of baking coming from the kitchen. The cinnamon and cloves and the vanilla that makes me always think of Mrs. Harmon's Christmas cookies." Yule breathed deeply, imagining he smelled the delicious aromas of the kitchen at Grandfather's estate in Hertfordshire. "So your family will be in London for Christmas?"

"Yes, through the New Year. Then we will move back home until spring when we will return for my and Charlotte's Season." Penelope tried to heft the heavy basket but had to settle for dragging it on the ground.

"Let me have that." Yule grabbed the handle and lifted it easily. "We don't want to dump it out on the way back."

Penelope stood with her hands on her hips, arms akimbo, giving him a perturbed look. "I could have managed, you know."

Yule grinned at her. "I know. But that's what you have me along for."

She uttered a disparaging sound that was totally charming, then joined him on the trudge back to the clearing. "Boys always think they know best, but so seldom do."

Chuckling, Yule glanced down at her. "And where in all your years did you acquire that piece of wisdom?"

"From observing the boys I knew in Ireland growing up. None of them gave me credit for having any sense either." She wrinkled her nose. "I had hoped things would be different now."

"Oh, I think you have sense, Penelope, just not the brawn it takes to carry this heavy load."

"I could have figured out how to do it, Yule."

"But you needn't bother when I had the solution right here." He raised the arm carrying the basket. "You could spend your time better occupied."

"Doing what?" She looked up at him, puzzled.

"Figuring out how to avoid getting kissed under the mistletoe during the game." He laughed. It ought to be fun watching her dodge and weave to avoid capture.

"Who said I wanted to avoid it?"

Yule halted dead in the snow. Penelope continued several steps ahead before she noticed he had stopped. What the devil did she mean by that? "But that's the object of the game."

She glanced back over her shoulder, a smile spreading over her face. "Are you sure about that, Yule?"

Unable to move, Yule stood still watching as Penelope continued picking her way through the snow toward the clearing, his mind devoid of thought other than the crystal clear idea that he was in more trouble than he had ever bargained for.

CHAPTER FOUR

GRINNING WIDER WITH every step, Penelope reached the clearing well before Yule put in an appearance. Pleased with how well her endeavor had worked out so far, she took a moment to congratulate herself on a plan well executed. Of course, she'd been arranging this first meeting with Yule for the past two years, ever since Mama began talking about Charlotte's come out. It had been her own suggestion that she and Charlotte come out together, ensuring she would be taken to all the entertainments and not left at home with a governess. Because how else was she to meet and enchant Yule Quartermain?

And things were progressing nicely. So far today, she'd done exactly what she'd set out to do. She'd talked to Yule respectfully, using his formal name as Charlotte had suggested. When she talked, she'd spoken with him about the approved topics, such as the weather and Mr. Dickens, which had worked admirably to further their conversation. And now she'd given him notice—thrown down the gauntlet, metaphorically speaking—that she was actively looking to get kissed during the Mistletoe Run. She'd shocked him, of that she was certain, but that wasn't necessarily a bad thing. At least he couldn't deny any longer that she was a young lady—an *eligible* young lady—one he could look on with an eye to becoming his wife.

Whether he *would* do that, of course, was still uncertain. But

Penelope would do everything within her power to make that happen. So, when she reached the clearing, where other guests were also straggling back in as well, she hurried toward their host's son, Fritz Kastner, smiling her sweetest at him. "Good morning, Mr. Kastner."

"Good morning, Miss Penelope." He returned her smile, his eyes lighting up. "How may I help you?"

"We are about to commence with the Mistletoe Run, are we not?" She glanced toward the growing number of people grouped over in the trees, all of them looking upward.

"Yes, as soon as all the guests have returned from the woods."

"Then my partner for the greenery gathering, Mr. Ulysses Quartermain, and I wish to be paired together for the first round of the run. If you can do that, Mr. Kastner, we would truly be very grateful." She smiled at him, batting her eyes ever so slightly.

"Uh, well, I will see if that can be arranged, Miss Penelope." The gentleman looked very uncertain. He glanced around the clearing and spied Yule, just coming toward them.

"I know the selection is usually random, however Mr. Quartermain and I are old friends and we have laid a wager on whether or not he will be able to catch me." She giggled and Mr. Kastner visibly relaxed.

"Ah, I understand, Miss Penelope."

If one mentioned the word "wager" with regard to a Quartermain, no one thought anything further of the matter.

"Yes, exactly. Thank you, Mr. Kastner. I appreciate your help with this." She turned just in time to see Yule setting the basket of cuttings down with the growing pile beside the waggonette. Swiftly, she rushed toward him, taking his arm just as he put the heavy basket down. "Mr. Kastner says they are making up the game right now. Over there." She pointed toward the guests milling around under the skeletal oak trees. "It seems we are just in time."

"Penelope, you didn't mean what you said just now, did you?" Yule's frown from the night before was back.

"Why would that be a bad thing, Yule?" Please, couldn't he simply give in and let her have her way? "That is what mistletoe at Christmas is for."

"When you're of a proper age for it, perhaps."

Anger surging through her, Penelope swung herself around so she stood in front of him, stopping him mid-stride. Her body fairly trembled in outrage. "And you don't think I'm of a proper age?"

His frown seemed more from confusion than anger. "No, I don't. And I can't understand why you think you are either."

"Because I *am* of a proper age, you ninny." What on earth was wrong with him?

Yule cocked his head, his frown becoming more pronounced, but before he could speak, Mr. Kastner appeared, grabbed their arms and propelled them forward.

"Come right along, now." He pulled them along the two lines of people, one only men, the other only women, standing or stamping their feet in the cold, until they reached the beginning of the lines. "The easiest way to make sure the two of you are paired together is to put you at the front of the line. You don't mind running first, do you?"

"What are you talking about, Fritz?" Yule pulled his arm out of his friend's grasp, then looked around, his face registering the horror of finding himself opposite Penelope, about to try to catch her as she ran under the huge green ball of mistletoe twisting in the cold breeze above them.

"Good luck on the wager, old chap." Mr. Kastner slapped Yule on the back as he hurried away from them. "On your mark."

Penelope glanced at Yule to find him glaring at her, his stare sharp enough to puncture her heart. At that moment, with his active malice directed at her, all she wanted to do was run as far and as fast as she could to get away from the wretched man who couldn't see that she wasn't the little girl he'd said goodbye to ten years ago. She was a woman, with a woman's feelings that he'd just trampled on as if they were of no consequence whatsoever.

"Get set."

Blinking back tears, Penelope turned her face toward the lane between the trees, where she intended to run like the wind and never look back. If she never saw Yule Quartermain again it would be too soon. She tensed, ready to—

"Go!"

With a cry, Penelope leaped forward, dashing away as though the hounds of hell were snapping at her feet, though they would have been much preferred to her true Quartermain adversary. Her half-boots slipped on the snow, causing her to wobble, but she found her footing and regained her stride. Listening keenly for his pounding footfalls, all she heard were the racing of her own heart and the *shush shush* of her own feet. Instinctively, she slowed and, despite her vow, glanced back over her shoulder.

Yule hadn't moved. He stood watching her, his face pinched, his brows in a deep frown.

So he wouldn't even chase her? He didn't want to get within yards of her, was that it?

Indignation flamed up in Penelope like a fire fed with dry wood and potent spirits. She whirled around, her hoops riding up allowing chilled air underneath her warm petticoats. The shock of that simply fueled her further as she stalked back toward Yule and the murmuring guests, taking in every bit of the spectacle.

"What's the matter, Mr. Quartermain? Have your legs no strength? Are you winded from lugging the greenery back to the clearing? I told you you should have let me do it." Penelope's voice carried loudly in the crisp air. "A young lady has quite enough stamina to prevail when older gentlemen discover they don't have the staying power they think they have."

Yule's eyes narrowed, but he kept his silence, which infuriated Penelope even further.

"Or do you fear I will simply outrun you? To make a poor showing in front of your friends might make you seem ridiculous." Penelope had slowed down until she stood about five feet in front of Yule, who hadn't budged. "What's wrong, Mr.

Quartermain? Cat got your tongue?"

"Behave yourself, Penelope," was all she got from him, in a low growl.

"Or what? You'll chase me?" She made a face, sticking her tongue out at him just as she'd done all those years ago when he and Victor had forbidden her to tag along to the fishing pond one day. "You couldn't catch me if you tried."

Without warning, Yule lunged toward her.

Penelope shrieked, and threw herself backward, circling around the pathway, as the crowd cheered her on. She dodged and wove back and forth, laughing as he came close enough to brush her sleeve before she nimbly skipped out of his reach. This was more like it. She twisted around the stump of a tree, putting it between her and Yule, her gaze darting here and there, trying to find a path to freedom. The only one left her was down between the rows of oak trees.

She turned to flee toward her only hope of escape when her heel caught on a half-submerged root. With a cry she fell, her arms going out instinctively to keep her hoops from tangling, guiding them to collapse under her as she'd been taught since she'd first graduated to grown-up clothing more than three years ago.

Strong arms embraced her before she had sunk a foot. Yule grasped her, his hands easily spanning the circumference of her waist and lifted her with an ease that took her breath away. Everything about him took her breath—the touch of his hands on her body, the nearness of him pressed right against her, the faint scent of his citrus cologne—until her lungs burned for lack of air. The rest of her burned as well.

He turned her around until she faced him, staring into the dark blue, no, almost black eyes as he studied her for several moments. The crowd had hushed until all she could hear were the beating of her heart and the whoosh of the wind through the trees.

Mesmerized, Penelope peered at him, wondering if he was

simply going to stand there holding her forever. Well, she wouldn't mind that at all. Her gaze strayed upward, past his face to the lofty oaks above them—and the large green ball with waxy, white berries clinging to it directly above them.

Penelope found her footing and pushed upward, sliding her arms around Yule's neck, and pressed her lips onto his, kissing him for the very first time.

Heat poured through her from her lips, down her arms, her back, her sides, all the way down her legs until her toes curled inside her half-boots. It was like she was electrified, with sparks shooting through her body and out her fingers and toes. Despite all these incredible feelings, she reveled in the fact his lips were soft, yet firm. And that he was incredibly gentle, despite everything they'd just gone through. Lord, but she never wanted this to end.

Yule broke the kiss and glared down at her. "What the hell have you done?"

HE'D KNOWN, AS well as he knew his own name or the fact that the sun rose in the East each morning, he should ignore Penelope's taunts. She wanted him to chase her, wanted him to catch her and kiss her. She'd admitted as much earlier. But he wasn't going to give into her childish ploys. Or so he'd thought until she'd stuck her tongue out at him. Why that action, so reminiscent of their childhood, would enflame him, he didn't know. However, the sight of her pink tongue mocked him in a way too visceral to be ignored. Before he could think to stop himself, he was after her.

The chase was exhilarating—as excited as a wolf must feel when hunting an extremely cunning rabbit. His heart pounded in his chest, his mind fully engaged in countering her every strategy, his arousal making his member stiffen alarmingly. Fixated on

Penelope, Yule heard nothing save his own ragged breathing and her squeals of excitement, each one making his cock harder. When she put the tree stump between them, he began to feint to the left in an effort to draw her toward the right, where he could finally grab her and end this madness.

Instead, she turned to run up the pathway between the oaks and tripped.

Without conscious thought, he bounded forward before she had even made it halfway to the ground, seized her about her waist and jerked her upright, then spun her around, ready to scold her like the willful child she was. When he gazed down into her beautiful face, however, all thought of reproaching her vanished. All he could do was look at her loveliness, her bright blue eyes with the eyebrows swooping upward like startled birds, the dusting of charming freckles over her nose, the enticing pink Cupid's bow of her lips and realize that what he wanted to do was kiss her senseless.

Before he could decide if he would in fact indulge himself in that particular lunacy, she struggled upward, slipped her arms around his neck and pressed her lips to his. The explosion of heat to his groin was instantaneous, and Yule froze, hoping against hope he didn't spill himself there and then. The unexpected rush of lust he felt for her made him pause, unable to decide if he should deepen the kiss or end it immediately before his baser instincts took over in front of the entire company of guests.

Laughter and the sound of clapping filtered into Yule's mind, clearing it immediately. Very carefully, he broke the kiss and put Penelope back on her feet. "What the hell have you done?"

He spoke as much to himself as to her, although the look of immense satisfaction on her face told him she knew very well what she'd just done.

"I'd say I won the game." She gazed up at him, triumph in every line of her face.

"That's an understatement." Yule glanced around as the rest of the company continued to laugh and chatter around them. He took her arm, to escort her off the playing field, then paused, looking back through the lines of guests awaiting their turn at play, which included Penelope's sister and his cousins Tom and Julius. God, but he was going to get a ribbing for this. "Let's go."

As he passed along the lines, heading them back toward the waggonette that would return them to the house, Fritz hurried over to him. "Are you all right, Miss Penelope?"

"I am fine, Mr. Kastner." She beamed at him and Yule felt a flicker of jealousy flair.

"I'm taking her back to the house, however—" He glared at Penelope when she looked about to protest. "—just to make certain she didn't turn her ankle."

"Very prudent, Yule." His friend nodded. "I'll instruct the driver to take you there directly." Fritz fell in step beside them. "So who won the wager?"

Yule shot a look at Penelope, who smothered a smile.

"I did, Mr. Kastner," she said, shaking with laughter.

"Congratulations, then, Miss Penelope." He eyed Yule. "To best a Quartermain at a wager is quite a feat."

"Yes, it is, Fritz," Yule growled. "And we have yet to discuss the method of compensation she will receive for it." He gave Penelope a warning glance. "We will attend to that in the waggonette on the way back to the house, won't we, Penelope?"

"Whatever you say, Yule." The demure answer was pure sham, but Fritz made no comment, merely gave the driver his instructions.

Yule helped her up into the wagon and they set out on the chilly ride back to the house. Silence reigned for most of the drive, Penelope sitting calmly across from him with that siren's smile on her lips. Why she'd decided to torture him in this particular way, he hadn't a clue. When they drew close to the house she ventured a comment. "Did you want to discuss the wager, Y—"

"There was no wager between us, Penelope." His words came out louder and harsher than he'd intended, but maybe she needed to understand just how angry he was with her. Why he was angry, however, was another thing, and not at all up for discussion.

"Of course there was. You wagered I was going to avoid getting kissed during the Mistletoe Run and I wagered I would not." She smiled broadly at him. "So, I won."

"That is not what happened, Penelope." Had she truly taken his comment as a wager? If she'd been born a Quartermain, perhaps then he'd agree she might have.

"Oh, but I think it was, Yule. And as I am the winner of the wager, I will exact my payment tonight, if you please." The minx grinned at him and his stomach dropped.

What the devil did she want him to do *tonight*?

"I will expect you to stand up with me for the first waltz at tonight's ball as payment, if you please." Her eyes sparkled and Yule let out the breath he'd been holding.

In his still heightened state of arousal, he'd been certain she'd say she wanted him to debauch her, although given the intimate nature of the Viennese waltz, her request was not far from the mark. They'd be dancing face to face, in very close proximity for an ungodly length of time. Still, her request wasn't as scandalous as he'd feared. There was nothing to stop him from agreeing to her request, save the overarching fear that the dance would in fact lead to much more intimate contact between the two of them.

"Very well, then." He had to agree to some payment, else he suspected Penelope would accuse him of backing out of the wager, and that he could not have, whether or not he thought it a legitimate wager. "The first waltz is yours, Miss Penelope." He glared at her, which only made her giggle. "But we will then consider the wager duly paid. Agreed?"

"Agreed." She nodded, but her eyes flashed in the bright sunlight, and she licked her lips, making his gut tighten.

No doubt about it. The waltz tonight would only be the beginning of the hell he'd have to pay.

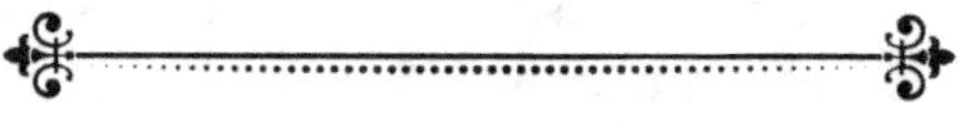

CHAPTER FIVE

THE DELICIOUS SCENTS of Christmas wafted across the Kastners' ballroom, two drawing rooms opened together that gave a large enough space for dancing couples. Long garlands of the bayberry tied with red ribbons, decorations of holly and rosemary accented with gold ornaments in each window sill, and green balls of mistletoe hanging at strategic spots overhead gave the room the festive air demanded by the season. Yule entered, immediately scanning the crowd for Penelope, who he assumed would descend on him like a streak of lightning to claim her prize. Amazingly, she seemed to not be present yet.

Breathing a sigh of relief, Yule strolled further into the room, nodding to acquaintances as he continued to glance around. Surely Penelope would not let her chance go by to dance the first waltz with him. What she hoped to gain from it, he didn't quite know. Had she set her cap for him? Rather an odd thing for a young lady not yet out to do. There were so many other eligible gentlemen here, although none quite so young as she. Still, her parents must have made it clear to her that she should dance and flirt with the younger set. After their dance, he would take her back to her mother and that should be the end of the matter.

Musing about who else he might ask to dance tonight, Yule jumped when Lady Augusta Hardy appeared at his side, quite out of breath. "Good evening, my lady." He bowed and smiled. "Are you running away from someone?"

"Of course I am, Mr. Quartermain." She fanned herself, peering about as if looking for someone.

Yule scarcely needed to guess who. "Is Julius pursuing you already this evening?"

"Not pursuing yet, no. However, I wanted to steal a march on him and engage you in the first dance." The lady's eyes snapped with thinly veiled anger, although why she was angry with his cousin, he wasn't certain. "So I don't have to refuse him yet again. It's becoming so tiresome."

"Well, you might think about accepting a dance with him then, my lady." Yule felt for his cousin, loving a woman who obviously did not reciprocate that affection. "It would be a change of pace at least."

"That would do nothing save prolong the agony, Yule. I mean Julius no harm, but I cannot lead him on to believe I will change my mind about him." Lady Augusta waved to a friend of hers, then turned her attention back to Yule. "I know it is quite scandalous for a lady to ask a gentleman for a dance, but will you dance the first with me, please?" She cocked her head bewitchingly. "You may call me Augusta, Yule. We have been friends for some time now. I think the proprieties may be dispensed with.

Suddenly, Yule completely understood his cousin's fascination with the lady. She was certainly beautiful, but then many women had beauty. She was dressed impeccably in a gown the deep orange color of leaves in the autumn, embellished with black lace and velvet ribbons that complimented her jet-black hair. There were, however, many ladies of the *ton* who dressed to the nines at every ball. No, it was all those things together, enhanced by her intelligence and keen sense of daring that appealed to him, and obviously, to his cousin. One might say the lady was trouble, however she gave off an aura of confidence in all she said and did that persuaded one that she had everything under control, whether she actually did or not. An enticing proposition, no doubt about it.

"I would be honored to dance with you, Augusta." He smiled and bowed again. "As long as the first dance is not a waltz. That I have promised to another."

She laughed, a triumphant sound that made Yule cringe. Had he just betrayed his cousin or not? A simple request for a dance shouldn't be a sign of disloyalty, but somehow the lady made him feel it was. "Excellent. Now I simply need to do the same thing with every other gentleman in the room save Julius."

"You shouldn't crow about it so, Augusta. Julius is a fine gentleman with a title and estates. If you'll pardon me, you could do worse than become Lady Boxtd." The least Yule could do was stand up for his cousin, as he spoke nothing but the truth.

"Oh, Julius is a fine gentleman, I will grant you that. And yes, he's titled and landed." She looked Yule straight in the eyes. "And not very interesting." The lady shrugged. "There it is. I will confess I find no fault with his character. He is a kind and generous man who constantly says and does all the right things." Augusta shook her head. "I simply need more in my partner for life than that. I want someone with a hint of danger or mystery about him. Julius, God bless him, has neither."

"As the saying goes, be careful what you wish for, my lady. Because you may in fact get it."

"You act as though that would be a bad thing, Yule." She laughed again. "Now I will tell you someone who *has* caught my eye, who does have an air of mystery and perhaps a little danger as well—Julius's brother, Mr. Price."

"Francis?" Yule's eyebrows shot up. "You must be joking. Francis is the more retiring of the two. He's not even here, although I know he was invited."

"And that's what makes him rather mysterious, don't you think?" Her eyes sparkled with excitement. "I mean, he's got to find a wife the same as the rest of you. But he doesn't even seem to be looking. I find that quite interesting."

"The last thing I heard him say on the subject was that he'd actually found a lady he wanted to marry, but she wouldn't agree." Yule stared pointedly at Augusta. "That sounds awfully familiar, don't you think? Of course, they are twins, after all. Why shouldn't their troubles be similar as well."

The lady looked perturbed, her dark brows dipping in a sharp V and her lips in a definite pout. "I have never given Julius any indication that I would accept his proposal. In fact, I've gone out of my way to make certain he knows I will not change my mind. I cannot help it if he will not take 'no' for an answer."

"Nor can I say why he still pursues you, Augusta. Unless it's that he's truly in love with you." Yule suspected that to be the truth at the bottom of Julius's stubborn refusal to give up hope of Lady Augusta. "If that is so, and you will not change your mind, then I am truly sorry for him."

Augusta's face seemed to turn somber at his words, but after a moment, she shook it off and her smile returned. "Can you tell me who the young lady is who is staring at us with daggers in her gaze?"

A sinking feeling in his gut, Yule closed his eyes briefly. Heaven help him. With a sigh, he opened his eyes to find Augusta grinning at him. "Where?"

She nodded to a group gathered across the dance floor, where Penelope stood with her sister and his cousin, Tom. "The one with the titian-colored hair. Quite stunning, you know. Your latest conquest?"

"Hardly," Yule growled. "I am not in the habit of seducing girls in the schoolroom." Augusta had obviously seen them kissing at the Mistletoe Run to assume such a thing.

"But she's not still in the schoolroom, is she? Else why would she be at a ball dressed so stylishly?"

Yule's gaze strayed again to Penelope, who was indeed dressed extremely fashionably. Her gown was of a pale peach silk that shimmered in the candlelight, frothy with a pleated trim that covered her modest bodice and swooped around the gown's skirt in dizzying loops. Her auburn hair, crimped and pulled up on top of her head with ribbons that matched her gown, blazed as though she wore a crown of fire. Yule caught his breath.

"You do know her, though?" August tilted her head, her eyes studying him intently.

"She's an old family friend." Sight of Penelope had caused havoc in his groin once more. Why did she affect him so every time he saw her?

"Indeed." Augusta's brows rose. "I would say she's something more than that."

"Just because you saw us kissing under the mistletoe this afternoon, there is no reason to think there is anything more going on." He had to tear his gaze away from Penelope else he would surely embarrass himself here and now.

"I don't know what you're talking about, Yule." She shook her head, her mouth pursed in annoyance. "I've never seen the young lady before tonight." Her brow smoothed out, replaced by an eagerness. "So you were caught kissing under the mistletoe? Do tell!"

"We were playing Mistletoe Run and I caught her underneath the ball." She'd caught him—there was absolutely no doubt about that. Augusta didn't need to know that, however. "You didn't see that? I could have sworn everyone did."

"I didn't venture out into the woods this morning as I suspected Julius would be going. No need to tempt fate."

Yule shook his head. He truly hoped he could persuade his cousin to move on from Lady Augusta before she broke his heart for good.

"Now tell me about the kiss." The lady sidled up to him, her eyes big and hungry.

"It was a mere kiss under the mistletoe, nothing more." How fortunate he could lie through his teeth with a straight face. That kiss had been much more than a chaste peck under the kissing ball.

"Well, you're no fun. I'd have thought when a handsome gentleman like you kissed an attractive lady like that, bells and whistles would have gone off." Augusta stared straight into his face.

Years of playing cards now came to Yule's rescue. He dropped any expression and assumed a blank countenance. "She's really much too young for her to affect me that way, Augusta." Perhaps turning the tables would get him off the hook. "Quite unlike kissing a more mature young lady might do." He gazed back at her, slowly bringing a smile to his lips. "We could go find a sprig of mistletoe and see what happens."

She laughed and lightly slapped his arm. "You'd never do that, Yule. Not while Julius is still interested in me. You aren't the type to compete with his own cousin. Unlike some we know." She nodded toward Penelope, who was now talking avidly with Tom. Nodding enthusiastically to him, she smiled, lighting up her whole face.

What the devil was Tom trying to do?

The obvious answer was ask Penelope for a dance, as he then offered his arm—which she took—and led her toward the dance floor.

Yule ground his teeth until his jaw creaked. From the sounds of the orchestra tuning up, the first dance would not be a waltz, so Penelope was within her rights to accept another partner, just as Yule was doing. Still, something about Tom's exuberance as he led his partner to the ballroom floor stuck in his craw. The situation was getting out of hand too fast for Yule to comprehend what to do, save go out on the dance floor and keep an eye on his rakish cousin. "Are you ready for that dance, Augusta? The orchestra is tuning up."

He turned to her to find her staring across the dance floor, not at Penelope and Tom, but at the couple standing next to them—Julius and Charlotte St. Claire. Yule stepped back, taking in the sight of Lady Augusta with undisguised jealousy on her face. Staring at the couple as though she wanted blazing arrows to shoot out of her eyes, Augusta clenched her jaw and fist at the exact same time. Yule would not have given Miss St. Claire very good odds of remaining alive had Augusta possessed a weapon.

What the lady's performance *did* do was give him a bit of optimism that Julius wasn't quite past hope for his suit just yet. He'd have to pass that tidbit along to his cousin. "Augusta?"

She shook herself and turned a terribly vivacious smile on him. "Shall we dance, Yule? You never gave me an answer to my earlier request."

"By all means, my lady." He offered her his arm and they headed out onto the dance floor. Neither one of them wished to be there particularly, but Yule didn't quite know where he wished to be, either. Did he want to dance with Penelope? She was a mere child. So, other than the dance she'd "won," he should be worrying about finding other suitable partners.

The only problem Yule was having at the moment, however, was trying to keep his gaze off Penelope and Tom long enough to take his position with Lady Augusta, which was going to make dancing this reel even more challenging than it would usually be.

CHAPTER SIX

ALMOST AS SOON as Penelope entered the ballroom, she was inundated with gentlemen asking her for dances. It was quite shocking to her, as of course she'd never had such attention bestowed on her before. She'd attended several parties back in Ireland last summer, but the young gentlemen there had been merely polite. She'd often not had a partner throughout the dances, so this flurry of gentlemen was quite invigorating for her self-esteem. Before she knew it, she'd agreed to at least seven dances, including an additional one with Lord Clavering who'd been dancing attendance on her ever since she entered the room. It had never occurred to her that parties could be so much fun.

Then she caught sight of Yule across the ballroom floor, laughing and talking animatedly with a statuesque lady with jet-black hair and a superior attitude. When she laughed along with Yule, Penelope couldn't help scowling at the pair. She hadn't waited all these years for Yule just to have someone else snatch him from her grasp.

"I hope you have saved at least one dance for me, Miss Penelope."

Startled, Penelope whirled around at the low, lovely baritone voice of Mr. Thomas Weston, Yule's cousin, to whom she'd been introduced last evening. Tall as Yule, with dark hair, vivid blue eyes, and a smile that would make a lady's heart flutter, Mr.

Weston was quite the most handsome gentleman here. "Of course, I have, Mr. Weston, if you are free for the first one, I hope."

"Luckily, I am." He flashed a smile, showing white, even teeth. "Is it a waltz, by chance?" His eyes darkened. "I love to waltz."

Penelope's face heated as her heartbeat suddenly quickened. "Ah, no, actually Mr. Kastner told me it's to be a reel."

"Then will you promise me the first waltz as well?" His voice lowered. "I would love to dance a waltz with you, Miss Penelope."

"Well, but..." Penelope tried to gather her wits. "I have promised the first waltz to your cousin Yule." She smiled tentatively. "It has to do with a wager, you see."

"Oh, far be it from me to interfere with a wager." Mr. Weston grinned. "However, if there is more than one waltz tonight, might you promise that to me as well?"

"Certainly." She'd love to dance the intimate waltz with this handsome gentleman.

"Thank you, Miss Penelope." He raised her gloved hand and kissed it.

Penelope blushed, the warmth of his lips sending shivers down her back. She glanced from Mr. Weston to the gathering of guests across the dance floor and caught an angry stare from Yule. Penelope caught her breath. Was he perhaps jealous of her talking with his cousin? She laughed harder, hoping the sound carried to Yule's ears. "You are most welcome, Mr. Weston."

His gaze followed hers, and his grin widened. "My cousin seems rather taken with you. After that kiss under the mistletoe this afternoon, I would have wagered a betrothal would be announced tonight."

"Oh, no, Mr. Weston. There's nothing between Yule and I." Her smile faded. "He's made that perfectly clear to me."

"I wouldn't be too certain about that, Miss Penelope. My cousin is, at this moment, staring at me as though he'd like to slit my throat." Despite his words, Mr. Weston laughed. "I think he's mad about you, but there's only one thing to do to make him admit it."

"What is that?" She held her breath.

"Make him jealous." The gentleman offered her his arm. "And the best and easiest way to do that is to let him see you enjoying yourself with me and with others as well." He sent her a mischievous glance. "We could wager on it, if you like."

"That would depend on what we would be wagering, sir." Penelope wasn't so enthralled with Mr. Weston that she didn't stop to consider what he might wish to wager for.

"How about this? If I can make Yule jealous, you'll agree to meet me under one of the mistletoe balls sometime this evening."

"That sounds awfully scandalous, Mr. Weston." Kissing under the mistletoe was expected at Christmas, however Penelope wasn't quite certain Mr. Weston's kiss wouldn't make the one with Yule this afternoon seem like a peck upon the cheek in comparison. "I would not wish to get myself compromised while merely fulfilling a wager."

"I promise not to compromise you, Miss Penelope. In fact, your mother can be witness to the kiss if you wish." The glee in Mr. Weston's face gave her no confidence whatsoever.

"What would I win should you not be able to make Yule jealous?"

"You may name your price, in that case, Miss Penelope." His blue eyes twinkled. "But I assure you, I will win the wager."

"Why are you so certain?" Of course, Mr. Weston did know his cousin's nature. But she knew how Yule felt about her.

"Because I can almost see steam rising from my cousin's head at this very moment." He nodded across the room and Penelope glanced at Yule. Sure enough, he was glaring at her and Mr. Weston with an intensity that gave her goosebumps.

"And how are you so sure you can make him jealous?" Delighted with this turn of events, Penelope could scarcely take her eyes off Yule and the young lady he was standing with. She'd give anything to know who she was.

"Because I know my cousin." He laughed loudly and grasped her hand that lay on top of his arm. "And he knows me. Shall we?"

He led Penelope onto the dance floor. "If you wish to enrage him even more," Mr. Weston said, his eyes sparkling with mischief, "call me Tom."

They formed a ring of eight dancers: her and Tom along with Mr. Kastner and Lady Diana Bascombe, Miss Garvey and Mr. Winslow, and Yule and Lady Augusta. Yule's eyes narrowed when he looked at her, and Penelope shivered with delight. A jealous man might easily turn into a devoted suitor. The orchestra struck up a lively Scottish reel and Penelope curtsied to her partner. Then the group of eight joined hands and moved spritely to the left, then to the right, then broke into couples for a left-hand star.

Tom's hand around her back was warm and strange, but the dance moved so fast it was there and gone again as they reversed, then turned to each other, his handsome face grinning into hers. From there, they all heyed around the circle, weaving hand to hand from one dancer to another until she took Yule's hand briefly as she continued on.

In that short contact, however, her hand stung as though an electric shock had travelled from him to her. Shaking her head, Penelope continued back to Tom and they turned several times until she was nearly breathless. She'd danced reels before, of course. They were very popular in Ireland, and their dancing master had taught her and Charlotte several different variations of the popular dance. Something was different in this dance, however. And that something's name was Yule Quartermain.

The eight of them joined hands and circled around the first lady, Lady Diana, while she showed off her reeling steps. Then she began to set to her partner, then to her opposite while the rest of the circle clapped and caught their breath. After she'd heyed with both those gentlemen, the circle began to rotate around her again, and she then set to and heyed with the other two gentle-men in the circle. Once she completed those steps, the second lady, Miss Garvey entered the circle and the steps continued in the same manner.

As Miss Garvey was setting to with her partner, Tom leaned over to her as they clapped, his mouth so near her ear, his hot breath seemed to singe her skin. "Yule is fit to be tied."

Penelope immediately looked across the circle to find Yule staring at her, his face darkened in a frown. She glanced back at Tom, seeing a smirk on his face. Perhaps it hadn't been the best plan, to make Yule jealous. Of course, he wouldn't like her showing favor to his cousin, although she suspected if she'd done the same thing with Lord Boxtd, Yule wouldn't have cared at all.

Oh, she was so confused as to how to make Yule like her, to make him want to court her. She'd taken Charlotte's advice, but it hadn't gotten her very far. She'd tried flirting with him and that had helped, but taunting him had ended in disaster, except it had gained her that kiss and soon a waltz. But even though Yule had agreed to those things, he still didn't seem at all interested in her, just jealous of her spending time with Tom. That wasn't the same thing as being interested or having affection for her, was it?

The dance had continued on and now, when the group cir-cled around, Penelope went into the middle of the circle. Smiling broadly, she performed her favorite reeling steps kicking high and side to side, even though her huge skirts hid the movements. Such a shame the rest of her set couldn't see her perfectly executed steps. Especially Yule.

Then she was setting to with Tom, swinging him around, then crossing the circle and setting to with Yule. When he took her arm to swing her about, he leaned close and whispered, "Watch out for Tom."

Penelope jerked back, her gaze going to Yule's face. What did he mean by that? Then they were weaving about in a hey and he managed to whisper more urgently to her, "He's a rake."

She went back to reeling, her mind circling around the warning he'd given her, all the while an excited smile on her lips. Was Tom Weston a rake? If so, she'd certainly heard nothing of it from her mother or anyone else during the house party. Still, she'd be on her guard should he ask her to go outside for a breath of air. As it was freezing out of doors, she'd have been aware of the ruse even without Yule's admonition. But her partner had done nothing so far save be respectful to her. Was it Yule's jealousy speaking slander instead of the truth?

She set two with the other gentlemen, then they all circled around again, repeating the section of dance they'd begun with until they swung their partners around in a dizzying turn, Penelope laughing up into Tom's face for what seemed like forever, until the music finally ended with a flourish. Breathless, Penelope curtsied to her partner, who seemed not winded at all, then he wound her arm through his and led her off the dance floor.

"You dance extremely well, Miss Penelope," Tom said as they wove through the throng of dancers. "I'd wager you learned to reel in Ireland."

"I learned to do everything in Ireland, Tom. I lived there from the time I was seven." Her breath was coming back, thank goodness. "And please call me Penelope. If I'm to call you Tom, you might as well."

"Splendid." His eyes sparkled. "Yule will be furious when I tell him."

"Do you like baiting your cousin so much?"

"It's rare anyone gets to do so with Yule. He's always so serious, so unwilling to let even the family get too close to him. So when I have the upper hand with him, I assure you, I will use it." He stopped beside her mother and sister and bent over her hand. "Thank you for a lovely dance, Penelope. I shall look forward eagerly to our waltz."

Mama and Charlotte looked askance at her, but Penelope merely nodded and curtsied. "You are welcome, Tom. I look forward to it as well."

He bowed to them all, then hurried away.

"Why are you calling Mr. Weston by his first name, Penelope?" Her mother's voice was urgent in her ear. "You have only just met the gentleman."

"Because he is Yule's cousin, Mama, and he asked me to." Penelope couldn't help following Tom's progress around the room. "He is so handsome and witty and has perfect manners. Perhaps I should set my cap at him."

"Lord, Penelope." Mama grasped her arm and pulled her backward. "He may be Yule's cousin and the grandson of a duke, but from what Mrs. Kastner has told me, he's also a very well-known rake." Mama dropped her voice to a whisper. "He's been entertaining women on his ship ever since August. Something about a wager with his grandfather, the duke."

"Goodness." Penelope glanced around the room eagerly, searching for Tom. She'd never known a rake before. Now that she did, she wanted to enjoy the experience of talking to someone everyone thought was scandalous. Even better, she would be dancing with him later this evening. Splendid. "Well, he did not attempt anything with me, Mama. He was a true gentleman."

Suddenly, she spied Tom, being towed none too gently over to the French windows by Yule. That was a conversation she'd give a lot to hear. Meanwhile, she'd best allay Mama's fears for her. Much as she liked Tom, she was much more interested in how his attentions to her had affected Yule. She suspected when Yule came to claim his waltz, she was going to find out.

AFTER RELINQUISHING AUGUSTA to her next partner, Yule made a bee line for Tom, who'd just taken Penelope to her mother and seemed to be meandering around the ballroom, totally unaware the wrath of God was about to be visited on him. Coming upon him from behind, Yule seized his cousin's shoulder, wrenched him away from the gentlemen he'd stopped to speak to, and hustled him out the French doors before Tom could put up a fight. He pushed Tom out into the cold night air, one lantern lit overhead to give them marginal illumination.

"What the hell is going on, Tom?" Yule advanced on his cousin, who had the good sense to get out of the range of Yule's fist.

"Other than you accosting me out of the blue, cousin? Nothing that needs concern you." Tom danced backward as Yule lunged toward him. "Temper, temper, coz."

"What the devil were you doing with Penelope St. Claire?" Yule stilled, looking for an indication which way Tom would feint.

"I was dancing with her, cousin. That is what one does at a dance, if you don't remember. Oh, but you must, because *you* were dancing with us *too*." He reached into his breast pocket and withdrew a silver case, opened it and put a cigarette into his mouth. Tom produced a match, struck it, and lit up the tobacco, creating an acrid smell all along the verandah. "At least you have won me the wager I proposed to the fair Penelope."

"What wager?" Yule could scarcely restrain himself from throttling his cousin.

Tom eyed him, too much glee in his face. "That I could make you jealous during the dance."

"I am not jealous of you and Penelope St. Claire." The very idea was ludicrous.

"She said you wouldn't be. But then why am I standing out here, freezing my bollocks off, talking about her to you?" Tom took a drag on the cigarette, as though taking warmth from it.

"Because I don't want you to ruin the girl. She's just got to London. She's not even out yet. We both know your reputation ever since Grandfather gave you that ship." Yule winced. The tales he'd heard of Tom and the women he'd entertained on board were more than scandalous.

"My reputation isn't going to hurt the young lady, and I

promise you, Yule, neither am I. I simply wanted to dance with a pretty girl this evening, and I must confess, I think she is the most beautiful one at the party." Tom grinned again, then let out a low whistle. "I was surprised she still had dances left by the time I got to her. She did say you had won a waltz in a wager."

"I did." Glad of it now, Yule nodded enthusiastically. "The first waltz in fact."

"Yes, I'd tried to get that one, but she's saving a later one for me." Tom grinned at him.

"Because of your wager?" Knowing Tom, the forfeit could have been worse.

"Oh, no. Just because I wanted to dance with her." Tom stubbed his cigarette out. "The wager was for a kiss under the mistletoe."

His cousin must have been expecting Yule's blow, for he ducked as Yule's fist swung through the cold air just where Tom's face had been a second before. "What do you mean you're going to kiss her?"

Tom had retreated down the verandah where the shadows were thicker. "It's a kiss under the mistletoe, Yule. It's nothing. At least, it'll be less of a meal than the kiss you gave her this afternoon."

Yule pursued his cousin, stalking him down the hollow, wooden verandah floor until he stood in front of him, arms crossed over his chest, his head tilted at a cocky angle. "It's only mistletoe, Yule. I won't be the first to kiss her under it this Christmas." His teeth showed as he grinned in the dim light. "You likely weren't the first either. Had you thought of that?"

Yule stepped back, the red rage that had consumed him dissipating somewhat. What was it about Penelope that drove him into such a frenzy of protective fury? "So you swear you don't have any designs on her?"

"I'm too busy sowing my wild oats for the next—" he paused to count, "—eight months. Of course," he said, sending Yule an impish look, "if she's still unmarried by August, I can't say I won't consider her wife material."

"Hands off, Tom." The growl in Yule's tone hopefully signaled to his cousin that he was serious.

"If I were you, I'd be saying that to Lord Clavering. He's been very attentive toward her ever since she arrived. You've much more to fear from him than me at present." Tom cocked his head. "So, you intend to marry her then?"

"Don't be ridiculous." Why were people so intent on marrying him off to Penelope? Couldn't they see—

"Why not? You are clearly besotted with her."

"What?" Yule hauled his arm back and let fly a punch that would have laid Tom out had it connected. His cousin, however, nimbly sidestepped the blow once more and started back down the verandah, trailing laughter as he fled.

Shoulders slumping, Yule waited a moment for his anger to cool. Tom knew how to goad him, no doubt about that. He'd have to make certain his cousin didn't bother Penelope any more tonight. If there was a wager for a kiss, then he'd stand witness to the paying of that wager—so it would be noted as satisfied.

He'd best return to the ballroom now. God knew when they'd play the first waltz and if he wasn't present, he didn't want Tom volunteering to step in and fulfill the forfeit in his stead. He wouldn't put anything past his scamp of a cousin, so he wouldn't give him the chance to slip something past him tonight.

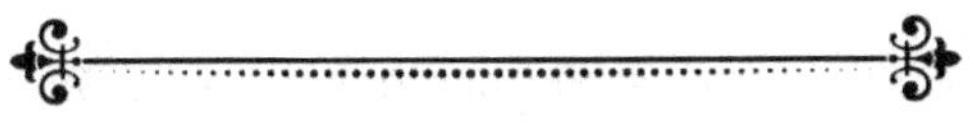

CHAPTER SEVEN

SHIVERING, YULE HURRIED back inside the ballroom, dazzled by the lights after the relative darkness of the verandah. When his eyes adjusted, he spied Penelope, standing beside her mother, scanning the room, brows furrowed in what was obviously displeasure. Then the strains of the orchestra caught his attention. They were playing a waltz. Damn. This was supposed to be their dance.

Cursing under his breath, Yule hurried around the already dancing couples, sprinted the last few yards and slid to a halt beside Penelope's mother. Trying to reclaim his flagging dignity, he smiled sheepishly at her. "Mrs. St. Claire, good evening. I'm dancing this next with Penelope."

"Good evening, Yule." The lady seemed to bite back a laugh.

He stepped up beside his partner, who glared so hard at him, it took him aback. "I believe this is the first waltz."

"You're late." Penelope grabbed his hand and pulled him back in the direction of the dance floor.

"I know, I'm sorry but—"

"Just shut up and dance with me," she shot back at him.

They reached the floor and Penelope stopped, tugged him into the position for the waltz, then looked up at him expectantly. "Well, you have to lead. Start us off."

Dutifully, Yule watched the twirling dancers, counted in his head, then started them off smoothly, blending them in-between the waltzing couples seamlessly. As they dipped and wound around the floor, Yule finally relaxed and glanced down into the face of his partner, expecting a smile. What he found was a perturbed expression.

"Aren't you going to apologize for your tardiness, Yule?"

Her question and irritated tone took him aback. Well, he could fight fire with fire. "You told me to be quiet, Penelope. I didn't think you wanted excuses."

"Not when I already know what your excuse was." She stared up at him from narrowed eyes.

"And what do you suppose it was?" Yule turned them so quickly, they almost careened into another couple.

"Be careful, please. I do not want us to take a tumble and become the laughingstock of the party."

"Don't worry. I am an excellent dancer." When he could keep his mind on the steps. But with Penelope in his arms, glaring at him as though he'd killed her dog, he was having more trouble concentrating than ever before.

"That remains to be seen." She squeezed his shoulder. "Now tell me what you said to Tom out on the verandah."

"Tom!" He spun her around so quickly, Yule himself became dizzy. "How dare the blackguard ask you to use his first name. You don't know him at all."

"Please don't do that again or I shall be wretchedly ill all over you." Penelope's jaw clenched and she looked rather pale.

"Should we go back to your moth—"

"No. I won this dance fair and square and I'm going to enjoy it, whether you do or not."

"As you wish, Miss St. Claire." If the child was going to act willful, he'd simply finish the dance and then return her to her mother so she could deal with her.

"Ah, you have resorted to formality with me. I'll wager you didn't stand on ceremony with your cousin." Although she didn't say Tom's name, Yule could still hear the familiarity in her voice when she spoke of him.

"I'm only trying to protect you, Penelope. Tom was always wild, but since my grandfather gave him that ship, he's been even worse." Yule hadn't even had to hear it from the gossip around town. Tom himself had boasted of his conquests several times. "I hate to say it, because he's my cousin, but decent women aren't safe around him."

"He was a perfect gentleman when he was with me." She flicked her gaze up at him and sniffed. "An excellent dancer as well."

"He was dancing with you simply to get my goat. And he knew the quickest way to do it was to flirt outrageously with you." Shaking his head, Yule suddenly could pay attention to the dance again. Tom wasn't interested in Penelope at all. He wanted to get back at Yule for some reason. And he had damn near done it, too.

"So you don't think a gentleman like Tom would wish to dance and flirt with me because he found me interesting and attractive?" The outrage in her voice captured Yule's attention just in time.

"I didn't say that, Penelope." Was she going to take offense to *everything* he said tonight? "He's older than you is all. And I know for a fact he's not looking for a wife right now, although..." Yule paused, about to tell her about the marriage wager. God, no. That was the last thing he should tell her. Alex said to be sure to tell the young lady he was going to marry, but he wasn't planning on marrying Penelope. And as she already seemed to be pursuing him, if she knew he was supposed to be looking for a wife, she'd be relentless in trying to get him to marry her. In fact, he needed to speak to his parents immediately and ask them not to reveal the wager to the St. Claires. Since Penelope didn't seem to know about the wager yet, they probably hadn't divulged it to her parents. But the two older couples appeared to be thick as thieves once more, so he'd best warn them as soon as this dance was over. And Tom and his other cousins. Lord, how was he ever to keep it from her?

"Mama says I should look for a beau who is older than me." She gazed off to the side of the dance floor, to the knot of bachelors where Tom was standing and laughing. "She actually said Tom was likely too young for me. He isn't mature enough."

"Well, in that one thing I have to agree with your mother." Yule shook his head and scowled at his cousin, though the rogue didn't seem to notice. "Tom is practically a child himself."

"Huh." Penelope snorted as they rushed past the area where Tom stood. "Either you are blind, Yule, or you are jealous of Tom flirting with me. He's not too young because he's past his majority. Isn't that the yardstick most of the *ton* goes by?"

"Well, yes…" Penelope was correct in that. Gentlemen who had attained the age of one and twenty were usually considered grown men, able to run their lives or their estates without any further fuss about it. Try as he might however, Yule couldn't envision Tom wishing to settle down, even for a moment. "If you put it that way, yes, he is a man. That doesn't necessarily mean he always acts like one."

Penelope mumbled something and though Yule bent his head toward her quickly, he couldn't catch it. "I beg your pardon, what did you say."

She shot him an exasperated look. "I said you don't always act like one either."

He had to get away from Penelope, if for nothing else than to stop all her wrangling. Still, he needed to warn her off his cousin, else he'd feel a cad if something happened to her. "Nevertheless, Penelope, you should watch yourself with Tom. You can ask around, but I'm telling you the truth about his reputation. If you were going to set your cap at someone next Season, it shouldn't be him."

"Perhaps I should set my cap at you, then." The sly look in her narrowed eyes sent a tremor through Yule. "Because you are certainly the more mature of the two of you, aren't you, Yule?"

His mouth dried as though he'd not had a drop to drink in a

month. "Please be serious, Penelope. I'm only trying to help you."

"I am being serious, Yule." She squeezed his hand and he almost stopped them right there in the middle of the dance floor. "There's no reason you shouldn't court me, is there?"

This was what he'd been afraid of. Shaking his head until his ears rang, Yule's first thought was he needed to end this dance and take the recalcitrant child back to her mother. "Don't be ridiculous, Penelope."

"Give me one good reason why you shouldn't?"

Yule swallowed hard and steered them toward the end of the dance floor. He couldn't believe Penelope was serious. Nor could he think how to answer her while he was maneuvering them around the floor. Once they commenced a balance step—something that needed absolutely no thought to execute—he could free his brain enough to answer her. "You are not even out yet, Penelope. I cannot court you. You're too young to be thinking about a serious courtship."

"I'm seventeen years old, Yule. Mamma brought us to London *because* I'm old enough to be out. Or will be in February." She peered into his face, pleading. "Why can't you see that?"

That pulled him up short. Ever since he'd recognized her last evening, all he could see was the little freckled-faced girl who'd tagged along behind him. He hadn't been able to make himself accept the idea that Penelope was a young lady now. A desirable young lady who other gentlemen might very well wish to dance with, or flirt with. Or court. "I can see that."

But somehow, not until this minute. Not even this afternoon, when they'd kissed under the mistletoe, had he given her a thought beyond friendship. At least not very much. One simply couldn't admit to being aroused by a lady young enough to be his—well, he wasn't old enough to be her father. Uncle, maybe? Older brother? It was deucedly awkward, whatever it was.

"I don't think you do, Yule." Penelope had stopped dancing and was looking up into his face, a determined look on her face.

He cocked his head, puzzled by the gleam in her eyes.

"I need to show you."

"Show me what?"

"This." She raised herself up on tiptoe, pressed her lips to his, and kissed him.

Once more absolute shock shot through Yule's body, from his mouth down to the tips of his toes. Heat engulfed him, as though the room had suddenly been lit up by a bonfire. Reason melted, the first casualty of the heat, and he found himself kissing her back, turning their heads so their mouths fit perfectly together. Time ceased to exist, giving way to the touch of her lips, the taste of her that made him hunger for more.

He might very well have tried for more, but the abrupt end to the music followed by the hushed clapping of gloved hands brought Yule back to his senses. Slowly, as though he was moving though molasses, he leaned back from her, his gaze taking in the rapt look on her face, as though she was Sleeping Beauty and his was the kiss that had brought her back to life.

Oh, Christ. That kiss. They were in the ballroom with at least fifty people watching. Penelope was ruined. And all the guests knew it. He'd been so worried about Tom debauching her, he hadn't given it a thought that he might be the one to do the deed. This was a nightmare from which it was impossible to awaken. "Do you know what you've done, Penelope?"

"I kissed you, Yule." Her laugh was playful, although this was no laughing matter.

"I compromised you, Penelope. In front of a room full of witnesses." He gazed about, expecting someone to come up and accost him over his treatment of her. No one, however, seemed to mark them at all.

"No, you didn't." She shook her head, setting her curls to bobbing.

"Penelope, a gentleman cannot go about kissing a woman in public, especially not like that, without dire consequences." They'd be forced to marry of course. The thought stopped his breath. He couldn't do that. He couldn't marry *Penelope*.

"Not when they're under the mistletoe."

Jerked back from his calamitous notion, Yule finally focused on Penelope, who was pointing to the ceiling. He craned his neck back and sure enough, a huge ball of mistletoe, thick with white berries, hung suspended from a bright red ribbon.

Relief poured through him like the flood waters in spring. "Oh, thank God."

"Not exactly the comment I'd hoped for, but I trust that kiss has finally made you aware that I'm a perfectly eligible young lady." She raised an eyebrow. "One you should absolutely consider courting."

Yule stared down into her fresh, eager face, a surge of lust rushing through him like a freight train. How he'd been able to ignore the fact that Penelope had grown up, he hadn't a single idea. It was as though he'd been wearing blinders these past two days—blinders that had suddenly been ripped off. He could now see what both Tom and Julius had tried to tell him. She was the most beautiful lady he'd ever seen, and although she could be annoying as hell when she wanted her way, the pull of attraction could not be denied any more. Not with his member straining against his trousers and his blood pounding in his ears. But he had to sort all these feelings out and the ballroom was not the place to do that. He grasped her arm and hurried her off the floor. "I need to take you back to your mother, Penelope."

"That's all you can say? After trying to kiss me senseless?"

He kept his eyes on the floor as he threaded them through the crowded room, but her tone said everything her words did not. Better to have her angry with him at this juncture than have to argue and try to explain the unexplainable. "Yes."

They fetched up at her mother's side and Yule bowed to both ladies, then turned and fled without another word. He ran out of the ballroom, down the hallway, into the library where he shut the door, then leaned against it, panting as though he'd finished a race. He doubted Penelope would follow him, but he still wished for a key to lock himself away. If he saw her again tonight, he wasn't certain he could keep his baser self in check. Having now seen her as an eligible young lady, he couldn't not think of her that way. Couldn't help wanting her that way.

Yule straightened and made a bee line for the decanter on the sideboard. Pouring a hefty dollop into the waiting tumbler, he sent a word of thanks to Fritz and his father for keeping such blessed libations at hand and downed the brandy at a gulp. The burning liquid comforted him, but did nothing to reassure him that his change of heart was a good thing where Penelope was concerned. The house party was over tomorrow, so he'd set off first thing in the morning, giving himself some time back in London to think this through before he did anything rash.

God knew he'd done enough of that this weekend.

CHAPTER EIGHT

Ten days later
December 24

THE FESTIVE AROMAS of bayberry and pine wafted through the Duke of Welwyn's townhouse, and every banister, windowsill, and railing was festooned with fresh greenery. Penelope stared upward at the huge chandelier in the great hall, each of its arms hung with a ball of mistletoe, her heart speeding up. Not only was the light fixture bedecked with kissing balls, but every entryway seemed to have at least a sprig of the innocuous plant hanging above it. After her last experience under the mistletoe with Yule, she had no idea how he might behave around her. Either he'd turn tail and run, or she was in for garnering a huge collection of tiny white mistletoe balls.

After the butler took their coats, Penelope and Charlotte and their parents were shown down the hallway to a huge drawing room that had also been decorated sumptuously for the season. Penelope gave a surreptitious glance upward and sure enough, there were mistletoe balls hanging all over the room. She'd need to be quick and careful if she wanted to avoid being kissed this evening. *If* she wished to do so.

The room was filled with Quartermains, from Yule and his three sisters—Cassandra, Phaedre, and Iphigenia—and their husbands and children, to several of the other cousins, including Julius and Tom. There were other people as well, who all chatted pleasantly as if they'd known one another for years. Her parents were heading toward the imposing silver-haired gentleman seated near the fire and the older lady sitting beside him surveying the room with obvious pleasure. They must be the Duke and Duchess of Welwyn, Yule's grandparents. She and Charlotte had been warned to be on their best behavior around them. As if Penelope would dream of offending a duke. She trotted dutifully behind her parents and curtsied to the distinguished couple.

"Happy Christmas, Mr. Ambassador, Mrs. St. Claire." The duke inclined his head toward them. "Welcome to Welwyn House. You have been absent from our company for far too long."

The duke and her parents droned on and Penelope sent furtive glances around the room, looking for Yule. He must be here somewhere…there! In the corner with Tom and some of his other cousins. She certainly hoped he wouldn't hide himself away with them all night.

"Miss Penelope."

She jerked her attention back to find the duke looking directly at her, an amused expression on his face. "I see your attention is exactly where it should be, my dear. On the young gentlemen. An excellent thing you've appeared when you did, Miss St. Claire, both of you." He nodded to include Charlotte. "All of my grandsons are looking to get married soon. I see no reason why it should not be to the daughters of our old neighbors." The duke's gaze seemed to pierce Penelope and she held her breath. Did he know she'd set her cap for Yule?

"My dear, you must not be so blunt with young ladies." His wife put a light but restraining hand on his arm. "I know you like to speak candidly to our grandsons, but Miss Charlotte and Miss Penelope have more modest sensibilities. My dears," the duchess continued in a soft and soothing voice, "why don't you run along and speak to Yule's sisters. I seem to remember you playing together when you were younger."

"Thank you, Your Grace, we did," Charlotte said, answering for them both, although Penelope had been much too young. Still, it would get them out of this awkward moment. They both curtsied again and Penelope followed Charlotte hastily toward the far side of the drawing room where an older lady who was surrounded by several other ladies was serving tea. There were other groups scattered around the room, none of whom Penelope recognized at all. Of course, she'd likely not met any of them when she was seven.

"Charlotte, is that you?" One of the ladies, who bore a passing resemblance to Yule about the eyes and mouth, looked eagerly toward Charlotte as they approached the little grouping.

"Yes. You're Iphigenia, aren't you?" Her sister's face lit up with a warm smile.

The lady patted the seat beside her on the chaise. Without a jot of hesitation, Charlotte sat and began talking easily to her old friend, leaving Penelope rather at sixes and sevens. She accepted a cup of tea from the lady she assumed was Iphigenia's mother and wandered to an unoccupied sofa in-between two of the groups of women. Eventually the talking would dry up and perhaps they would play some games.

"Good evening, Penelope."

She jumped and turned, amazed to find her sofa now occupied by Tom Weston, grinning from ear to ear. "I should have you all to myself for at least two minutes. Long enough for Yule to discover where I am and come throw me out on my ear."

"He'd never do such a thing in the duke's house." Penelope was aghast and thrilled at the same time.

"Oh, none of us hold Grandfather in the awe most people do. Neither does our grandmother. She rules him with an iron fist." Tom laughed and cut his gaze back over to the knot of his cousins in the corner. "I think he's just seen us. I'd best be prepared to run. I hope to partner you during one of the games this evening."

"What games?" It wasn't dancing, but games could give couples a chance to talk privately if they kept their voices low.

"Oh, the usual ones—Charades, The Minister's Cat, Blind Man's Bluff." Tom leaned over to her and said in a husky voice, "If I'm it, I know who I'm going to try to find."

Lord, Yule was right. His cousin was incorrigible. She'd best keep her distance from him tonight. The last thing she wanted was to end up the talk of the party tonight or worse—the talk of the *ton* tomorrow. "No peeking, Tom. You have to play fair."

"I doubt he can do that, Penelope." Yule suddenly towered over them and Tom jumped to his feet, his grin widening.

"I told her three minutes at the most. You are so predictable, Yule." He bowed to Penelope. "Lovely to see you here tonight, my dear. I hope to see more of you later."

Laughing at Yule's indignant look, Tom headed back to the group of cousins, leaving Yule to stand over her, staring at her as though he wished to reprimand her but didn't quite dare. Before he could speak a word, she patted the seat next to her. "Won't you have a seat? You and Tom are the only people I know here. Well, and Julius a little."

"You didn't know my sisters when you were younger?" With a look around the room, Yule lowered himself carefully onto the sofa.

"I was seven. They were young ladies." Penelope shrugged. "They were Charlotte's friends. You were mine." She looked up at him. "You and Victor. Lord, but I missed him even more once we went away. You and him." She lowered her voice. "Then I didn't have anyone left at all."

To her surprise, Yule smiled at her. "You had Mrs. Philpotts."

Penelope's heart gave a great leap. He remembered Mrs. Philpotts. "I did have her, thank goodness. And thank you, Yule. I couldn't thank you properly when I was a child, but I can say a heartfelt thank you now. Mrs. Philpotts went everywhere with me. Whenever I was lonely, she was my companion, just as you said she would be when you gave her to me."

"I'm very glad to hear that, Penelope." His smile was laced

with tenderness. "Very glad you had one friend when you went so far away."

Why couldn't he be this wonderful all the time? Penelope dropped her gaze, suddenly bereft of a conversational starter. What had Charlotte counseled her to talk about? Literature. "I've just finished reading Dickens's *A Christmas Carol* again this year. I read it each Christmas to put me squarely into the Christmas spirit."

Not the best segue into a topic, but it was the best she could do with her nerves fraying further by the minute.

"Is that a favorite of yours then?" He seemed distracted and Penelope couldn't decide if she was diverting him, or simply off-putting to him.

"It is a favorite at Christmas, although during the rest of the year, I must profess a fondness for *Oliver Twist*." She giggled. "Such an adventurous orphan."

"And such a villainous villain." He sent her a side-wise look and waggled his eyebrows, sending Penelope into further peals of mirth.

"Oh, yes. Bill Sykes is a terrible man. He makes Fagin seem positively saintly by comparison." She smiled pleasantly, dreading the lengthening silence that progressed after that last salvo. "Though Mr. Scrooge in *A Christmas Carol* is both villain and hero. I think that rather clever of Mr. Dickens. Don't you?"

Yule rose abruptly. "Would you like some punch?"

Penelope blinked. He shouldn't have answered a question with a question. What was wrong with him now? "Yes, please. Thank you."

"I'll be just a moment." He strode off toward the serving table where footmen were constantly coming and going with trays of drinks. Why hadn't he simply waited for the footman to bring the drinks to them?

"You're 'it,' Penelope."

She jumped as Tom appeared out of nowhere. "For goodness sakes, Tom. Announce your presence before you make me swoon from fright." Not that she could be angry at the handsome, grinning face. "What do you mean, 'I'm 'it'?'"

"We've decided to play Blind Man's Bluff and I volunteered you to be It." The glee in his face made her sigh and wonder what might happen if she felt for this gentleman what she did for Yule. Life might be very different. Unless he truly was the horrible rake Yule painted him. With his boyish smile, it was very difficult to think of him as a debaucher of women.

"Why didn't you volunteer yourself? And who's 'we?'" She thought she knew, but it was always better to know more rather than less in these games.

"My cousins and I. We all agreed it would be much more entertaining if a young lady were the first one to have to find a victim." He nodded toward the corner where several gentlemen were still huddled.

"Oh, very well." She didn't mind being the first victim. The game was amusing and hopefully this would be her only turn as "It." "Where are we to play? I don't want to knock into the duchess's fine China."

"We'll play down at the far end of the room. There's less to break there." He grabbed her hand and began towing her toward the spot where his cousins stood. "Penelope is willing, gentlemen. I told you she would be. Who's got a clean handkerchief?"

The gentlemen began hunting in their pockets and Julian pulled his out first. "There, Miss Penelope. I believe that will do. Shall I tie it on for you?"

"Isn't anyone else going to play?" She looked at the little groups where her sister was talking animatedly with the other ladies. "We don't want to be rude, surely. Will someone invite them to play?"

"Julius?" Tom raised a brow. "I did my part."

"Very well." Julius started toward the others and then her eyes were covered.

"Stand still while I tie this on you." Tom's voice was so close to her ear, she almost jumped.

If he wasn't flirting with her, he was giving a convincing performance of it.

"Now we turn you three times..." He put the words into action and spun Penelope, not quickly, but enough to disorient her. She'd glimpsed where people were standing before the handkerchief descended, but her head was spinning now and she had no idea where anyone was standing. He released her and she wobbled a moment, getting her bearings, then took a hesitant step to the right.

Pray God she didn't bump into a priceless urn or a crystal vase. Her mother would lock her away in her room for a year. Another tentative step to the right, then she stopped and listened carefully. There was conversation still going on, but it was farther away and she managed to disregard it. Concentrating on sound alone, she began to discern slight noises—rapid breathing, the creak of the floorboards, the subtle rustle of clothing as someone shifted position.

Suddenly, Penelope lunged toward the place where she'd heard the floor screech. A burst of laughter and the shuffling of shoes on the carpeted floor said she'd been close. Carefully, arms outstretched, she circled to her right, listening with all her might. A sudden rush of air to her left made her turn that way and spring toward where she believed a person was standing.

She fetched up against a hard, masculine chest, the fabric under her fingers soft and expensive. The gentleman grunted and rocked backward. There was a soft curse and Penelope gasped. "Yule!"

Tearing the handkerchief off her face, she stared up into his disapproving face, brows lowered in a frown, mouth pursed. In his hand he held a dripping cup of punch, a puddle of the beverage at their feet. "Oh, dear. I'm so sorry. I didn't know you'd come back."

"Of course, you couldn't know." He shot a glare over her head, and she turned to find Tom grinning at them broadly, as though he'd orchestrated the whole thing.

A footman scurried forward, took the cup from Yule, and bent to scrub at the carpet.

"I'm so sorry about your coat." She pointed to his jacket where the punch had made a large round stain.

"Don't worry about it. I'll go upstairs to change." Yule stared at his cousins then shook his head. "I likely will simply retire. Tomorrow will be a long day, I suspect." He bowed and turned to go.

Miserable, Penelope tugged at his sleeve. "I'm terribly sorry I've ruined your evening."

"Nonsense." He shrugged. "You haven't ruined it. I will see you tomorrow." He continued toward the doorway, each step wrenching Penelope's heart.

Tossing the handkerchief in Tom's direction, she picked up her skirts and hurried after his cousin. "Yule."

He stopped, just at the doorway and turned back to her.

Breathless, she rushed up to him. "I…I…" So many emotions swirled around her, it took a moment to form a sentence. "I'm dreadfully sorry for spilling the punch on you." She looked up at him, his face wiped blank and unfathomable. "You will forgive me, won't you?"

He glared down at her, a dark hunger in his eyes she'd never seen before. Frightened and thrilled, she couldn't tear her gaze away.

Then his mouth was on hers, and she forgot everything—the punch, his jacket, her apology, the entire audience of his cousins—except his lips on hers, soft but insistent until her very bones threatened to melt.

Then he broke the kiss, turned and strode down the corridor.

Dazed, Penelope turned toward the cluster of people who had just witnessed a kiss that had undeniably compromised her. She cleared her throat, trying to put off the moment of reckoning as long as she could. Tom's grin was about to split his face in two, to say nothing of her sister's shocked countenance. If Mama hadn't seen that indiscretion, she'd hear about it as soon as

Charlotte ran over to her.

Straightening her shoulders, Penelope raised her chin and caught a glimpse of the only thing that stood between her and ruin. Composing her face into a pleasant smile, she pointed upward, to the small ball of greenery that hung in the middle of the archway. "Mistletoe." She widened her smile. "Merry Christmas, everyone."

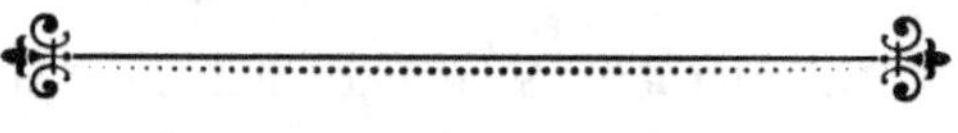

CHAPTER NINE

WITH LEADEN FEET Christmas morning, Yule descended the main staircase at his grandfather's townhouse where the whole family had spent the night. God, he wished he hadn't promised his grandparents he'd stay or he'd have slunk off last evening to his digs in St. James. Now he'd have to run the gauntlet of his cousins' cracks at breakfast, unless he wished to starve. He entered the breakfast room and, just as he feared, all three of his cousins were already wolfing down the eggs and kippers. For a moment, starvation seemed the better choice and he started to back out of the room.

"Yule!" Tom had glanced up just before he could make his escape. He leapt to his feet and hurried toward him. "Just the man we wanted to see."

The others at the table—his sisters and their husbands, his parents, aunts, uncles, the whole damn family it seemed like—ceased their talking, looked toward him and Tom, then burst into animated chatter as his cousin led him down to the seat he'd apparently been saving for him. Tom pushed him into the chair and sat down beside him. "So, when's the wedding?"

The withering look he gave his cousin only made Tom's grin grow wider. "And a Happy Christmas to you too, cousin. But, no, there is no wedding planned, as I'm certain you know."

"After that kiss you gave her last night, I'm not certain of that at all." Tom grabbed a croissant and lathered it with butter. "Wouldn't you say, Julius? Francis?"

His twin cousins rolled their eyes in unison.

"Neither should you be certain of it, cuz. If her father hadn't been so preoccupied with Grandfather that he missed it, I think he'd be insisting you make an honest woman of Penelope this minute." Tom bit off the end of the bread and chewed with gusto. "About time too. I'm surprised no one has told him you've been kissing her every chance you get since they arrived from Ireland."

Yule bristled at that. "That is absolutely not true, Tom. Stop spreading rumors like that or you'll have me called out, if they still do that these days."

"It's not a rumor, Yule, and you know it. You kissed her most thoroughly during the Mistletoe Run at the Kastners', then again on the dance floor at their ball. Last night's spectacle makes three—and those are just the ones I've witnessed. God knows what you've been doing in private."

"Nothing. We've been doing nothing at all in private." Thank God for that. They'd done enough in public. "It's just been kissing under the mistletoe, for goodness sakes. Everyone does that."

"Normally kissing under the mistletoe is a quick peck on the cheek or maybe a brush of the lips." Tom looked at him askance. "You two have ventured toward the indecent for couples who are married, much less betrothed." He took up a forkful of kippers. "Which you also are not."

Yule gritted his teeth, then nodded to a footman who set a plate down in front of him. Since he had chosen the inquisition over starvation, he'd better dig in while he still had an appetite.

"Why is that, cousin?"

The stealthy question came just as Yule had put a heaping forkful of eggs and kippers into his mouth. Glaring at Tom, he chewed silently, trying to formulate an answer that wouldn't make him sound like a fool. At last, he swallowed and wiped his lips. "I didn't think it appropriate to court a lady a young as

Penelope."

"But you think it's appropriate to kiss one that young?" Julius leaned toward him, a smug smile on his face. He'd apparently been taking in every word of the conversation.

"I…Well…of course…" He was damned if he did and damned if he didn't. "No, I should not have been kissing her like that, but…" Yule sighed. "You don't know what she's like, Julius."

"What do you mean?" Francis stuck his head around his twin's.

"And here's another one poking his nose into my business." Yule picked up his coffee, the rich aroma soothing him as he sipped.

"Don't be like that, cuz." Francis frowned. "I haven't met the lady. What is she like?"

"She's a siren, that is what is," Yule exclaimed, unable to contain the name of the image he'd had all night of Penelope as one of the naked women in the painting by William Etty that had haunted him for years. "Beautiful and alluring, yet unattainable except at great peril."

"Wait, what?" Tom looked at him, bewildered. "I understand she's beautiful and alluring. But unattainable? Penelope adores you, Yule."

"She's too young, Tom." That fact had haunted Yule during a night when he'd thought constantly about Penelope, naked and in bed with him. Having spent ten days away from her, he'd begun to think of her again as little Penelope.

The puzzled look on all his cousin's faces mystified him.

"What are you talking about, Yule?" Julius finally spoke up. "You've said before you were surprised she'd grown up, but children do that. You do realize she's not a child anymore, don't you? That she's the exact age of marriageable young ladies."

Yule shook his head. "I suppose I do realize that, Julius. Sometimes, at least." He could scarcely explain it to himself, much less someone else. "I managed to see her finally as a very desirable lady at Kastner's ball. But I haven't seen her since, so

I've reverted to thinking of her again as the little girl who tagged along after me and Victor."

"Well, you didn't seem to have any trouble distinguishing one from the other under the mistletoe last night," Tom chimed in again. "You must have feelings for her."

"Of course, I do." Too many feelings by far. And all of them contradictory.

"Have you told her that?" Francis pushed back his chair. "Perhaps we should adjourn to the drawing room. We're to meet the rest of the family there when they have done with breakfast to open presents. Perhaps we can steal a march on them to sort this out for Yule in private before they converge on us."

"Good idea, brother." Julius tossed his napkin down and rose, as did Tom.

Yule looked lovingly at the remaining kippers and eggs. He was going to have to run the gauntlet anyway and without a proper breakfast. Scooping up one more forkful of kippers, Yule popped them into his mouth quickly, blotted his lips, then rose and followed his cousins from the room. If they could help him sort out this business with Penelope, he'd be happy to forfeit breakfast.

They settled quickly into a corner at the far end, away from the enormous Christmas tree, its fragrant candles in the process of being lit by the footmen. Christmas swirled around Yule, the wax of the candles, the holly, bayberry, and rosemary greenery that surrounded the entire room. The overwhelming essence of home and family engulfed him, making him long to have such a feeling surround him not just at Christmas, but every day of the year.

"All right, Yule…" Julius sat in an oversized armchair, like a king overseeing his subjects. "Why have you not declared yourself for Penelope? You are obviously very attracted to her. She's extremely eligible and seems to like you."

"Well, there's no accounting for taste," Tom quipped as he plopped himself down on a nearby sofa.

"Tom, you're not being helpful." Francis seemed ready to take the lead in the proceedings. "Yule, do you or do you not hold some affection for Penelope?"

"Of course, I do. I've always liked her." But he knew full well what his cousin meant. Did he have romantic feelings for her? That was something he'd scarcely admitted to himself, much less anyone else.

"As much as he's been kissing her, I'd hope to God he at least liked her." Tom grinned at Yule, obviously loving every minute of his cousin's discomfiture.

"That is enough, Tom." Julius looked threateningly at their youngest and wildest cousin. "We don't have much time before the others arrive. Yule, confession time. Do you have feelings of a romantic or serious nature toward Penelope? Yes or no."

"Yes." He could admit that much at least. He did have romantic feelings toward the dazzling young lady he still thought of as the little girl next door.

"Do you intend to do something about this or will the young lady be fair game for any of the rest of us?" Julius looked at him carefully.

"Hell, if you don't want to court her, I will." Tom bounded up from his chair. "She's the prettiest lady I've seen since summer."

"And Tom's not the only one who's interested in her." Julius crossed his arms over his chest.

"What, now you're wanting to court Penelope too?" Yule suddenly felt threatened by his favorite cousin. "What about Lady Augusta?"

"Not me, Yule." His cousin shook his head. "Lord Clavering."

"That is true, Yule." Tom's demeanor had sobered dramatically. "He was mad for her at Kastner's. Absolutely besotted. Worse than you, if you can believe it." He glanced at Julius and Francis who nodded gravely.

"It's true, Yule," Francis added. "I belong to the gentleman's club he just joined. The *on-dit* is he's about to make an offer for her with Mr. St. Claire. He's just waiting for the holidays to be over."

"No!" Yule shot up out of the chair as though he'd been launched from a catapult. He couldn't let that young whippersnapper swoop in and steal Penelope away from him just like that. Not when *he* loved her. Lord, he *did* love Penelope. His body was afire every time he saw her enter a room. His eyes sought her out, wherever she was, whoever she was with. And the thought of never being able to be with her because she was someone else's wife was absolutely unbearable.

He looked around at his cousins. Every eye was on him.

"I...I do intend to do something." He cleared his throat. "I'll go speak to her now."

A collective sigh of relief went up from his cousins.

"About bloody time," Tom said under his breath.

Giddy with the thoughts of what he was about to do—declare himself to Penelope St. Claire, the little girl who'd turned into the siren next door—Yule stalked out of the drawing room, heading toward a whole new world. God help him now.

CHRISTMAS MORNING HAD dawned crisp and cold. The windowpane in the room Penelope shared with Charlotte had frost on it. Penelope smiled and blew her breath on the ice-covered pane, then wiped it with the sleeve of her gown. She'd been up for hours, thinking about the kiss Yule had given her last evening before he'd disappeared. Had he known they were under the mistletoe? Or had he done it for a totally different and much more exciting reason?

Oh, but she had to find a pretext for them to call on the duke and duchess before her family left after the new year. They were to travel to Hertfordshire, back to her father's ancestral estate once the tenant left, and there await the Season in the spring.

What she'd do if Yule left town, she simply couldn't bear to think about.

A knock sounded at the door. "Come in," she and Charlotte called at the same time. Her sister was having the finishing touches put on her hair for the short trip downstairs to their small Christmas tree, decorated rather sparsely as they'd none of their real Christmas decorations with them. Everything on this year's Christmas tree had been made by hand or improvised by Penelope and her sister and mother. Papa had insisted it was the loveliest tree imaginable, but he was simply being nice. Perhaps next year, all their Christmas things would be back at their home. What Penelope didn't want to contemplate was that perhaps next year she'd be celebrating Christmas in her own home with her own husband. The trouble with that vision was that she had no guarantee whatsoever that the husband would be Yule.

"Miss St. Claire, Miss Penelope. Mr. and Mrs. St. Claire are insisting you come downstairs now." The stern voice of their housekeeper, Mrs. McGraw, came through the stout door loud and clear.

"Yes, Mrs. McGraw," Charlotte called. "We will be down directly."

"Do you have any idea what Mama and Papa have gotten for your Christmas present, Charlotte?" Penelope always loved giving and receiving presents on Christmas. She loved anything that made the house feel cozy and festive.

"I'm hoping it's that pearl necklace I've been longing for for my come-out ball in April. It will look so elegant on me, don't you think?" Charlotte arched her neck, as though the necklace were already lying there waiting to be admired.

"You will be the darling of the Season no matter what necklace you wear." Penelope smiled at her sister's happy reflection in the mirror. "I am quite certain the other young ladies won't hold a candle to you."

"You will be my greatest competition, Pen." Charlotte rose and pulled her warm rose-colored shawl over her shoulders.

"Don't think you won't, my dear."

"I only hope—" Penelope couldn't say it, not wanting to tempt fate. She truly hoped she wouldn't need a Season at all if only Yule would make a declaration.

Charlotte gripped her hand. "He will come around, Pen. If he doesn't by the start of the Season, I'll have a word to him myself."

"And what will you say to him, Charlotte? Marry my sister or else I will beat you about the head with my reticule?"

Charlotte broke into giggles, and Penelope joined her as they headed down the stairs. "Well, I shouldn't be so violent, Pen, but I'd do something to knock some sense into him."

Still chuckling, they entered the drawing room where the makeshift tree sat atop a large table ablaze with candles, presents piled underneath it. Penelope stopped to admire their handiwork—despite the fact they had had to make the decorations quickly, the tree looked very pretty indeed—then continued toward her parents who were speaking to some gentleman she didn't know was here. Who would be calling on Christmas—

Penelope stopped mid-stride, recognizing the back, the set of the shoulders, the style and color of the hair that could only be… "Yule?"

He whirled toward her, his face transforming from dignified lines to a boyish grin that stretched wider and wider as he beheld her. "Penelope. Happy Christmas."

At a loss for words or thoughts, she made a weak try at a smile and finally summoned the only thing she could say. "Happy Christmas."

"Yule came over this morning to speak to you, Penelope." Mama's eyes were huge and shining. She shifted from one foot to the other, as though she could not stand still. "Would you like to show him into the small parlor? Alice has laid a fire in there."

Still unsure this wasn't as vivid a dream as the ones Scrooge had had, Penelope nodded, then led Yule into the snug little room where they had been receiving the friends and family who'd come by to welcome them back to England. "Would you like to sit down?"

"No, I think I'd better stand for this."

She looked up at him, brows furrowed. "For wha—"

Without any further warning, Yule sank his mouth down onto hers, startling her so badly she had to grab onto his arms to keep from falling to her knees. His lips were firmer than the last time they'd done this, more insistent as well pressing against her mouth. The closeness of his body, the warmth they generated together was startling. Her whole body seemed to be heating to an amazing degree, tingles running up and down her arms, her legs, her spine. Along with those sensations came a strange urgency growing in the middle of her, something she'd never experienced before. Her head began to spin and Penelope feared she was on the verge of swooning right there in his arms when he broke the kiss. And though she was sorry, she could at least breathe again.

Penelope looked up at him, his eyes shiny and black as jet, and all she could think to say was, "There isn't any mistletoe in here."

He chuckled and tucked a stray tendril of hair back behind her ear.

The merest touch of his fingers on her skin made her burn.

"If you answer what I'm about to ask you correctly, we'll never need mistletoe again."

Penelope caught her breath. Was this really happening? Was she dreaming? "Do...do you want to court me, Yule?"

Slowly, he shook his head and Penelope's hopes crumbled. Lowering her head, she fought against the tears that pricked her eyes.

He put his finger under her chin and raised it up until she couldn't avoid looking into this smiling face. "No, Penelope, I don't want to court you. I want to marry you."

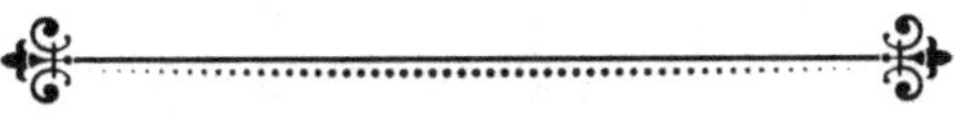

CHAPTER TEN

THE LOOK OF wonder that came over Penelope's face truly made Yule's heart melt. Her eyes widened, her mouth opened to a perfect little O that was as touching as it was erotic. All he wanted to do was scoop her up into his arm and kiss her senseless again, but he couldn't. Not until she gave him an answer.

After what seemed like an eon, she closed her mouth and swallowed hard. "Did you just ask me to marry you?"

"Yes, I did, sweetheart. And I'm waiting for your answer." It had to be yes, else he didn't know what he was going to do. He'd been a blind fool at Kastner's, had squandered the opportunity to claim her openly there, and had thereby almost lost her to that puppy Clavering. Thoughts of what might have happened had he not come to his senses this morning made him almost physically ill. Thinking of the years to come without this beguiling creature in his life was all but unimaginable. He continued to stare at her, willing her to say something that would put him out of his misery.

Penelope gulped at last, and shook her head, as though coming to herself. "Does my father know?"

"I asked his permission not long before you came downstairs." An inkling of alarm trickled down Yule's back, leaving him cold. He'd anticipated a joyous and emphatic "Yes," not this measured response from her. "He has given it. Wholeheartedly."

"You truly want to marry me, Yule?" There were tears brimming over her eyes and he longed to wipe them away, make them cease all together.

"Truly, I do, Penelope. It took me more than a little while to realize it, but yes, I do." He took her hand and squeezed it. "More than anything I want to marry you so we can be together always."

She looked up at him, her eyes still shiny with tears. "Oh, yes, Yule. Yes, I will marry you." She threw her arms around him, hugging him fiercely. "I've wanted to marry you all of my life."

"You have?" That was curious. He'd have thought Penelope would have forgotten him completely once she got to Ireland and started a new life. She had only been seven years old. He wouldn't have thought she'd have remembered him at all.

"Of course. You gave me Mrs. Phillpotts, remember?" She looked up at him, an endearing little smile on her lips. "The little doll I took to Ireland so I wouldn't be lonely." She squeezed him again. "Only someone with a kind and thoughtful heart would have known I'd need a friend. And I needed one badly, Yule. After losing Victor and you, I didn't wish to make friends again. I didn't for a long time after we settled in Dublin. Mrs. Phillpotts was my constant companion."

Yule cupped her face, amazed at the smoothness of her skin in his palm. "Well, I hope you won't mind me being your constant companion from now on."

"Of course! You have been all along, in my mind. Every time I looked at my doll, I remembered you and the fun I had with you and Victor." She took his hand and Yule's heart swelled. "As I grew older, my dream became to meet you again, have you fall in love with me, and marry me." Her face lit up in a brilliant smile that made her glow with beauty. "And now you have."

"Yes, I have. With some help from you." Had she not been so insistent, he might not have recognized the treasure right there in plain sight. He tilted her face up to his. "I'd like a little more help now, if you don't mind."

"With what?" Her frown made her nose wrinkle. He'd not noticed that before.

"This." He lowered his head until his lips touched hers, then slowly, gently, their mouths met fully. When he'd kissed Penelope before, Yule had been so focused on wanting to get away from her, he'd not taken the time to enjoy the experience thoroughly. Well, he was certainly enjoying it now. This kiss was wreaking havoc in his nether regions, no bones about it. His cock was making a valiant effort to escape his trousers, and Yule had to restrain himself from giving into its demands. His blood seemed to be on fire, licking though his veins, searing him to the bone until he could think of nothing but Penelope, his siren, naked in his bed. He pulled her to him and, unthinking, thrust his tongue through her lips.

Immediately, she stiffened in his arms, made a little sound of resistance, and began to pull away from him. With a sigh, he let her go. His future bride might look like a siren, but she had much to learn about how men and women pleasured one another. And he'd be her oh, so patient teacher.

"What did you do, Yule?" She stared up at him with wide, accusing eyes.

"I kissed you, Penelope." He had to bite back a smile at her outraged look.

"You never kissed me like that before." The charming frown was back.

"We were kissing under the mistletoe before." Yule glanced upward. "As you pointed out, there is none here. This was a much more serious kiss, a grown-up kiss between people who are betrothed." He raised an eyebrow. "Did you not enjoy it?"

Her frown deepened, as though she was thoroughly contemplating his question. "I did and I didn't. I mean, I did, but when you put…" Her cheeks turned rosy red. "What you did at the end, that startled me. You'd never done that before. It was…strange." She touched her fingers to her lips, as if that would help her explain her feelings.

"It won't seem strange after a while." He took her hand and wound it through his arm. "In fact, I suspect you'll come to enjoy it quite a lot."

She looked doubtful but nodded. "I suppose I will. But where are we going?"

Yule had started them toward the door. "I thought we should go tell your parents that we are officially betrothed."

"Goodness, yes." Penelope began to tug him, urging him to walk faster. "They will wonder what we have been doing all this time."

"Well, as I spoke to your father about this, I'm certain they know exactly what we've been doing." He chuckled at her once more outraged face.

"Yule Quartermain, you think they know that you've been kissing me like…that?"

"Well, they knew I was going to propose, and as one thing follows the other…"

She began to sputter, so Yule did the only thing he could think of to distract her—he placed another swift but chaste kiss on her lips. "Do not worry, my dear. Now we are betrothed, such things are very much allowed. We need to get to know one another better before the wedding." And oh, he wanted to know Penelope better in every way possible.

"I suppose if it's allowed…" She gazed up at him, her eyes slightly darkened. "Then we should spend lots of time together."

"My thoughts exactly." They were headed into the big family room now. "So I thought perhaps a carriage ride this afternoon would begin to let us become better acquainted."

"What an excellent idea!" She squeezed his arm and Yule felt it all the way down to his boots. Damn, but they'd better persuade her parents to agree to as short an engagement as was socially acceptable.

"Mama, Papa, Charlotte." Penelope's joyous voice filled the room with her excitement. "Yule and I are betrothed."

Of course, the announcement had come as no surprise, though there was much hugging and kissing between Penelope and her mother and sister.

Mr. St. Claire shook Yule's hand. "We can see to the settlements later this week, my boy. We're ever so happy to have you in the family."

"I am as well, sir. And I'm certain my family will be thrilled to know we will now have a closer connection."

"Mama, Papa, Yule wants to take me for a carriage ride this afternoon. That's allowed now, isn't it?" Penelope returned to Yule's side, taking his hand possessively.

"Yes, of course it is, my dear." Mrs. St. Claire sat down and indicated the sofa next to her. "Won't you have a seat, Yule?"

"I think I must return home to inform my parents, ma'am. They will want to hear this news as soon as possible. But I'll return at two o'clock for that carriage ride." He kissed Penelope's hand and she blushed.

"I'll be waiting," she said, breathlessly.

That little catch in her voice went straight to Yule's groin and he had to suppress an urge to groan. "So will I."

TRUE TO HIS word, Yule's carriage arrived at precisely two o'clock in front of the St. Claire's townhouse. In moments, Yule was out the door and running up the steps. He was about to knock when the door opened and there stood Penelope, dressed in a very fashionable red carriage dress decorated with rows and rows of flounces, and a pert bonnet with a large red and white striped bow tied under one ear.

"I just couldn't wait." She grinned from ear to ear. "I've been watching for you for the last half an hour."

"You look like a Christmas treat." Indeed, she made his mouth water. He offered his arm, which she took with a fierceness that surprised him.

"And you look very dashing, sir."

Wanting to look his best for Penelope, he'd changed into a more dapper ensemble for their ride. His newest suit was a fashionable green and blue plaid, which he wore with a white shirt and dark blue cravat. "I am glad you approve, my lady."

He ushered her into the carriage and gave the driver directions to head for the park. "I thought we'd begin in Hyde Park, then branch out through the fashionable parts of Mayfair and St. James. I can show you where my digs are, and then we can pay a call on my parents and grandparents at Welwyn House." He chuckled. "They are just dying to see you and gush over my fiancée."

"My parents are simply thrilled. We sat and talked a blue streak after you left. So much to think about and do." She settled back in the seat beside him, her arm and breast resting against him familiarly.

Yule swallowed hard and tried not to think about how close she was and how much he wanted to kiss her this minute.

"I think six months is scarcely time enough to get everything done."

He jerked his head around to peer down at Penelope. "Six months?"

"Yes, Mama has said that a six-month engagement is plenty of time to make the arrangements for the wedding, but when she began listing all the things that must be done, I cannot help but believe that it will take longer than that." She looked up at him, the little frown he so adored furrowing her brow. "Don't you think so?"

Aghast at the plan, Yule kept a smile on his lips, his mind feverishly working on a way to countermand a half-year betrothal. "If my family and yours work together, I think we could dispense with such a long engagement, Penelope. They aren't really necessary, are they? The point is that we are married and can begin to spend our lives together."

"Well, that is true, Yule. That is the main reason for the wedding." She gazed up at him, her face wreathed in smiles. "But don't you wish to squeeze every moment of joy out of our betrothal? We can be seen about town together, we can go to parties together, dance every dance together." Her cheeks grew rosy. "We can kiss…and you can show me that strange thing you did again." Her eyes sparkled and his cock gave an answering surge. "You said I would like it eventually. So the more we practice—"

"Oh, good God." Yule could not resist her. The feeling of her body pressed against him was enough to send him spiraling upward like a shooting star. The wide-eyed innocent stare, the Cupid's bow mouth poised for a kiss, the faint, sweet scent of violets that clung to her pushed him to grasp her shoulders, turn her toward him, and pull her perfect mouth up to his.

He noted her surprised "Ah" but no resistance as he pressed his lips to hers, then stealthily pressed his tongue to the seam of her mouth.

She hesitated, then slowly parted her lips.

More slowly than before, he slid in, his leisurely pace an agony for him, but he was determined not to frighten her again. Besides, they had all afternoon in the carriage. Gently, Yule began his exploration, trying to make the experience as pleasant as possible for her. He circled her tongue, then hesitated to see what she would do.

Subtly, Penelope leaned into him, her tongue moving in little circles, just as his had done.

Elated that she no longer seemed afraid of the sensation, Yule gave her time, hoping against hope she'd experiment a bit before he took the lead again. That patience was rewarded when she slipped her tongue into his mouth, making him groan with the pleasure of it. His member was now making itself known, but he could take care of that later. He wanted to savor everything Penelope devised to do to him. God knew they'd have to get inventive if he couldn't find a way to make Mrs. St. Claire agree to a much shorter engagement.

Emboldened, perhaps by his groan, Penelope chased his tongue around and around, pressing more insistently with her hands against his shoulders. In response, he slipped his arms around her, pulling her to his chest until her breasts were pressed snugly against him. Exquisite torture, but oh so delicious at the same time.

She strained against him, her tongue stilled, but her body urging itself toward him. Her hands slid up around his neck so that she lay on top of him—all of her atop him.

For once, he thanked God for women's fashions that encased them in a cage crinoline, else Penelope would be able to feel every inch of the desire she'd instilled in him. His cock was fighting to free itself from his pants. Well, that was a battle it must lose today, for certain. And every other day until he could marry Penelope.

Almost hesitantly, she broke the kiss and looked deep into his eyes. "That time was *much* better than the first."

Yule groaned. She would be the death of him.

"Did I hurt you?" Her worried frown had returned, even more charming now.

"No, sweetheart. Why would you think that?"

"You moaned just now, and earlier as well. I thought, perhaps, I'd done something wrong and it had hurt you." She tried to rise off him, but he held her tight to him.

"Not at all. You have given me pleasure is all."

"Kissing makes you groan with pleasure?" She shook her head. "That doesn't make any sense, Yule."

"Then tell me how our kissing this time made you feel? You said it was much better. That must mean you took some pleasure in it?" He was certain if he could get her to understand the world of pleasure that awaited her in the marriage bed, she'd be a willing accomplice in trying to hurry the wedding date.

"Well, yes, it wasn't quite so strange this time. And lying down on top of you like this makes me feel...tingly inside." Her whole face turned bright red, and she cast her gaze downward, unable to look him in the face anymore.

"Tingly, how?"

Again she tried to sit up, and Yule let her go, hoping to encourage her to explain.

"I can't explain it exactly." She cut her eyes at him. "I don't think it's proper for me to be talking about such things."

"I'm going to be your husband soon, Penelope. You can tell me anything. And I can tell you." If he wanted an ally, he had to take the chance. "Kissing you and having you lie on top of me like that made me feel tingly as well."

"Really?" Her eyes flew open wide.

"Yes. And more than tingly." He grasped her hand and pressed it to his trousers, where she couldn't help but feel his rampant cockstand. "Very much aroused."

Her mouth flew open, and he thought for a moment she might scream. Instead, her face turned indignant, brows straight, eyes staring at him as she tried to remove her hand. "Yule! What are you doing? Stop that!"

"I only wanted you to see what you do to me, Penelope. What power you hold over me."

"What do you mean?" Suspicion was there, but curiosity as well.

"The tingles you felt will get stronger as we become more intimate." He cocked his head. Their engagement might have been too recent for her mother to have given her instructions. "Has your mother talked to you yet about what married couples do?"

"No, Mama hasn't." Penelope waited, looked away. "But my sister Charlotte told me some things just now as I was dressing to come out with you."

"Your sister?" Yule was shocked to his boots. "But your sister isn't married yet, is she?"

"No, she's not. But she has been talking to several matrons since we returned from Ireland, and they told her quite a few…things that married couples are allowed to do." Penelope sighed. "I don't think they meant any harm, Yule. We are both going to be married soon. Why must such things be kept such a secret?"

"That's just the way Society is, my dear. Young ladies are supposed to remain ignorant of the more intimate side of married life until they are about to embark on matrimony. So please don't tell anyone else you know about such things. At least, not until we are closer to our wedding date. So perhaps your sister shouldn't converse with these ladies anymore. Nor should you, if you have been introduced to them."

"I have, Yule. But I'm afraid it's going to be rather difficult not to converse with them." Penelope's mouth twitched.

"Why is that?" Surely Penelope could refrain from speaking to these ladies. "Not that you have to give them the cut-direct, but simply eschew their company, my dear."

"I'm afraid I cannot do that, Yule." His fiancée seemed almost gleeful in her refusal.

"Why not?"

"The matrons who spoke to Charlotte were your sisters."

"What?" The innocuous motion of the carriage suddenly threatened to make him shoot the cat. "My sisters have given you and your sister instruction on…"

"Not everything, I'm sure, my dear." Penelope patted his arm. "They were aware of the impropriety of the situation however. If you recall, Iphigenia has never taken the rules of society much into account."

In that Penelope was completely correct.

"And Cassandra said that since Genny was telling tales, she had to have her share." Penelope nodded her head. "Again, you know them better than I do."

"I suppose Phaedre insisted on putting her tuppence worth in as well." His fiancée grinned and Yule groaned again. "So you likely know a fair amount about things no young lady should."

"Not a fair amount, but enough to recognize some of the

things we did." She looked pointedly at his hand. "Like what you just showed me."

"Then you must know how much I desire you, Penelope." Given the circumstances, honesty seemed the quickest route to capitulation. "And I hope you have felt a somewhat similar desire for me."

She nodded, hanging on every word.

"Then I hope you will help me in my quest to persuade your parents to allow us to marry in three weeks instead of six months." Even the normal time it took for the banns to be read would be a hardship for him, but much preferable to half a year of purgatory. He took her hand again and kissed it. "Will you help me, my love?"

"Oh, yes, Yule." She threw herself into his arms. "We will make Mama understand that we do not want to wait." Penelope laid her head on his chest. "Do not worry, my dear. I am certain, between the two of us, we can find a way."

Yule gulped as his member began to rise again, as it seemed to do whenever Penelope touched him. Yes, even three weeks would be an eternity of sweet agony. At least he could console himself with the knowledge there was an abundance of cold water to be had this time of year.

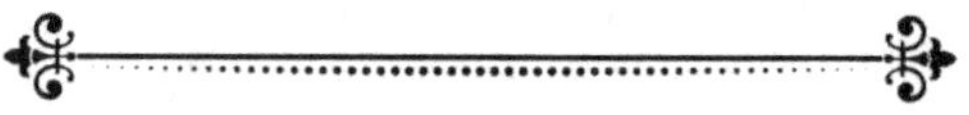

CHAPTER ELEVEN

"A BSOLUTELY NOT, YULE." Mrs. St. Claire shook her head so vehemently, the curls hanging beside her face threatened to put out an eye. "Penelope must have a formal engagement period, so that we may plan the day in style. And nothing is so beautiful as a June wedding, with all the roses in bloom. You can't wish to deprive her of this, I'm sure."

"No, ma'am, I would deprive Penelope of nothing, I assure you. It's just that we've been so long apart, we wish only to be together now." Yule's patience with his future mother-in-law might reach its limits soon. The woman had been arguing with him incessantly for the past half an hour and showed no signs of relenting.

"And there you have it." The lady crowed as though he'd agreed with her. "You have not seen one another for ten long years. You must take the next six months to become better acquainted again."

Biting back a groan of frustration, Yule shot a look at Penelope, dutifully helping her sister wind yarn. She wrinkled her nose at him, as if to say "I told you so", then turned back to whispering with Charlotte.

"I have just received an invitation to a special dinner from your grandmother, to celebrate your betrothal. I am certain it will be the first of many we can expect from family and friends." Mrs.

St. Claire looked smugly at him. "Another reason to keep the engagement a full six months from now. Think of all the entertainments at which you will be the guests of honor. You won't want to miss such celebrations all spring long, will you?"

"Certainly not, Mrs. St. Claire." Yule had to restrain the sarcasm in his voice, but the only celebrating he wished to do was with Penelope in his bed. Immediately. Still, he supposed he'd have to endure it if he wanted to marry his siren. And he did want to marry her. Very badly.

"Will you attend the pantomime with us tomorrow afternoon, Yule?" Mrs. St. Claire poured more tea into his cup.

"Yes, he most certainly will," Penelope spoke up from the sofa. "We love the Christmas pantomimes Yule, and haven't seen a proper one in ages. In Dublin, there were wonderful puppet shows at Christmas, but not an actual pantomime." She extracted herself from the yarn and hurried over to stare down at him with liquid blue eyes. "So yes, you must go with us. Please?"

These Christmas entertainments didn't interest Yule in the least, however if Penelope wished him to attend with her, he absolutely would. The more time spent with her the better. "Of course, my dear. I will gladly come along if you like."

"Good." She sent him a triumphant look and squeezed his shoulder. "We have planned to attend the one at The Princess's Theater. They're playing *Robinson Crusoe or Harlequin Friday and the King of the Caribee Islands*. Doesn't that sound thrilling?"

"I assume it's based on DeFoe's *Robinson Crusoe*?" Yule had read the book as a boy and thought it a corking good tale at the age of twelve. It might make a pleasant afternoon's entertainment if he was allowed to sit beside Penelope.

"Yes, I've heard it is." She slid down onto the seat next to him. "Won't it be such fun? And just think. We will be together all afternoon."

"That will be an absolute joy." Although he could think of other ways they could spend the time that would be even more joyous.

"I suppose that is why Penelope insisted on attending the panto at the Princess." Charlotte sniffed, putting her yarn ball down. "I cannot imagine any other reason to endure any performance lasting five hours."

"Five hours?" Yule's heart sank.

"Yes, but it will be such fun, Yule," she whispered softly, leaning close to him.

He could think of other things that were fun to do, although not in a theater. Perhaps he could enlist his siren's aid and make the afternoon absolutely memorable for the both of them.

⟫⟫⟫✲⟪⟪⟪

"THIS WAY, YULE. We are in the Dress Circle, just down there." Penelope motioned to a set of seats two rows from the balcony's railing, her face full of excitement.

Yule couldn't help but smile at his fiancée's enthusiasm. She'd been all atwitter ever since he'd whispered his plan to her as she'd escorted him to the door yesterday afternoon. Fortunately, her family's carriage wouldn't accommodate him and the family, so he'd arranged to meet the St. Claires at the theater. "Those are excellent seats, my dear. We should be able to enjoy the performance thoroughly."

"Oh, I'm certain we will." Following her parents and sister down the steps, Penelope stopped a moment, her hand going to her head. She winced.

"Is something wrong, my dear?"

"No, it's nothing." She waved her hand, as if shooing away a fly. "Come along. We don't want to miss the beginning."

They continued down until they found their seats, Yule thankfully positioned on the end.

"I told Papa to let you have that seat," she said as they sat. "So much more room for your legs." She gave him a knowing smile, then touched her temple again.

"My dear, are you quite all right?"

"It's nothing. I...I think all the excitement has given me a headache, is all." She patted his hand. "I'm certain it will...Oh!" Penelope grabbed her head in both hands.

Her mother caught the motion and turned toward her. "Penelope, what is the matter?"

"A headache, Mama." Penelope rubbed her temple, her brows furrowed.

"Is it very bad this time?" Mrs. St. Claire's voice sounded worried.

"I'm not sure. I hope it will pass, though." The doubt in her voice was absolutely genuine.

"Have you had these headaches before?" Yule asked.

"Sometimes, yes. Oh, dear!" Her cry was louder this time, making several patrons' heads turn toward them.

"It must be another megrim." Mrs. St. Claire looked alarmed. "James," she said, turning to her husband, "we must go. Penelope has one of her sick headaches."

"Oh, no, Mama. You should not have to miss the pantomime because I am ill." She winced again.

"But you need to lie down in a darkened room. You know that's the only thing that helps." Mrs. St. Claire gathered her reticule in her hands. "Come along, James, Charlotte."

"No, Mama." Penelope turned hopeful eyes on Yule. "Yule will take me home, won't you?" She looked at him hopefully.

"Of course not." Yule was on his feet in an instant. "I do not mind at all, Mrs. St. Claire."

The lights in the theatre flickered, signaling the start of the show.

"Well," Mrs. St. Claire looked first at Yule, then intently at Penelope. "As you are betrothed, there's no reason you cannot take her home, Yule. If you will see her inside the house, her maid can tend to her until we return. The megrim will likely have subsided by then. They come on suddenly, but don't always last long."

"I'll put a vinegar cloth on my forehead, Mama. That always helps too." Penelope rose and grasped Yule's arm to steady herself. "Please enjoy the show and be sure to take in every detail so you can tell me when you get home."

"I will, my dear." Her mother settled back into her seat. "And if you are no better when we return, we will send for the doctor."

"I'm certain that won't be necessary, Mama." Penelope smiled bravely and they turned to go.

Carefully, Yule escorted her up the steps. "Are they looking at us?" he asked, sotto voce.

"Yes, Mama is looking this way. Here, I'm going to stumble. Take my arm." Penelope staggered toward Yule, and he caught her as they climbed toward the exit doors.

"I think that will do the trick." Yule opened the door and ushered her out into the lobby. "Let me send immediately for my carriage." Yule snagged a passing usher and made his request, then they headed down the main staircase to the entry hall. "Perhaps we can see another pantomime later in the week. I don't want to deprive you, my dear. But I truly wanted to spend the time with you, not watching a performance for five hours." They stood at the main doors, peering out.

"Oh, but I don't mind at all, Yule." She flashed him a seductive grin. "I want to spend the time with you as well."

Her dazzling smile made his cock take notice. Again. "Let us stand outside the doors and wait for my carriage." The cold air might help restrain his baser urgings.

They continued outside, dodging around latecomers scurrying into the theater.

"This way, my dear." Forgoing some decorum, Yule put his arm around Penelope so she would not be buffeted by any theatergoers rushing to claim their seats. She leaned into him, sending waves of heat searing through him. He repressed a groan. Her nearness never ceased to arouse him.

At last, his carriage arrived and Yule opened the door, the steps rattling down immediately, and he all but picked Penelope up and put her in the conveyance. He bounded up behind her and took his seat beside her. "Now where shall we go, my love? We have at least four hours before we need to head to your house." He called to the coachman, "Start out into traffic, Lewis. I'll let you know where to in a moment."

The carriage jolted forward, and Yule settled back in the seat, fumbling for a blanket to tuck around Penelope. "Is that better, my dear?"

By way of reply, she turned toward him, her eyes snapping with excitement. "Very much better, Yule." Then she slipped her arms around his neck and pulled his face close to hers.

Stunned, Yule could say or do nothing save stare down into the beautiful face of the woman who would be his wife as soon as humanly possible and wonder what she would do next.

"EVEN BETTER NOW." Penelope kissed him, pressing her body against his in the most abandoned way she could think of. Yule's plan to steal some time together—going for sweets in the market or riding together in the park—was excellent. However, she wanted to make the most of every single stolen moment. If they were going to be thieves, then they must aim for the highest prize.

At last she broke the kiss and Yule managed to pull her arms away from his neck. "Penelope, what are you doing?"

She shot him a triumphant grin. "I thought you'd know what I was doing, Yule. You taught me."

Groaning, Yule firmly set her back on the seat and slid a little farther from her. "This is not the way proper young ladies act."

"Then I must be different than all the other young ladies you know, Yule." She bounced on the seat, then settled back in it and gave him a saucy smile. "And I think that's why you want to marry me. Because I *am* different."

"I cannot say you are wrong, my love." He grinned at her and edged close enough to put his arm around her shoulders. "So, what would you like to do with the rest of our afternoon?"

She leaned closer to him, her chest brushing his arm, excitement snapping in her eyes. "I think you should compromise me."

Yule froze, squeezing her arm in a vise-like grasp. At last he blurted out, "You mean here in the carriage?"

She giggled. He could be so literal sometimes. "No, silly. That would be very uncomfortable, don't you think?"

He gave her a strange, sidewise glance, then hastily said, "Yes, it would."

"But another place, like a bed, say, would be very pleasant, don't you think?"

Now Yule looked as though he was suffering a megrim. "What gave you this idea, Penelope?"

"Well, your kisses, for one thing." She leaned toward him, but he backed away. "You've been teaching me all about that, and each time you kiss me…" Quick as a snake, she darted over and gave him a hard peck on the lips. "Or I kiss you, I feel those tingles I told you about. Those very pleasant tingles. Then, of course your sisters have helped me quite a lot to understand what happens when a husband and wife engage in carnal embrace."

"Carnal embrace?" Yule's face got a pinched look to it.

"That is what Charlotte said Iphigenia called it."

"She would." He cocked his head. "What has she told you that makes you want to 'engage in carnal embrace' with me before we are married?"

"Well, for one thing…" Penelope spoke slowly, trying to get her thoughts into a coherent frame. "What Iphigenia said about…how it was done, made me…curious. It sounded awfully funny at first, but the more I thought about those tingles, I decided perhaps it might be quite nice indeed." She leaned toward Yule, and this time he allowed it until her head was resting on his chest, so wonderfully comfortable. "And if you compromised me, then Mama and Papa would have to let you marry me right away." She snuggled deeper into his chest. "And then we could do this all the time." She looked up at him and her cheeks heated. "This and…the other things."

Yule shook his head, although Penelope didn't think he was saying no… "Do you know the risk we would be taking?"

"We're already engaged, Yule. All we would be doing is what they used to call 'anticipating the wedding night' by a little bit." She wrapped her arms around his and leaned her head back on his shoulder. "Like getting a head start in a race."

"We would be anticipating it by six months, Penelope."

"Not when Mama and Papa find out. Then we'd only be anticipating it by a week at most." She hugged his arm and Yule groaned She'd wager his resolve was slipping.

"Your mother is going to be extremely disappointed and likely very vocal about it."

"Mama can't say much of anything publicly. She wouldn't want to risk damaging my reputation, and Charlotte's by association." Penelope shrugged. "Mama has another daughter who can have a long, decorous engagement with parties all around town."

"By that time, we might even have the promise of a grand-child to offer your parents by way of appeasement." Yule sounded almost convinced.

She smiled in what she hoped was a seductive manner. The Quartermain girls hadn't said much about seducing a gentleman, but Penelope had garnered things at her mother's afternoon teas in Ireland when Mama didn't know—or forgot—Penelope was listening.

It must have worked, because Yule rapped on the carriage's trap. His coachman opened it and looked down at them. "Yes, my lord?"

"There's been a change of plan, Lewis. Head for The Grafton if you please."

"Very good, my lord." The trap snapped shut, leaving Yule and Penelope in silence.

After a good long moment, Yule turned to her. "Are you certain, Penelope?"

"I am." She squeezed his arm again. "Aren't you?"

"I'm certain I don't want to have to take cold baths for the next six months."

"Why would you ever do that, Yule?" Why would anyone in their right mind wish to take cold baths?

"Part of a ritual gentlemen bachelors must endure until they are married."

"I don't understand."

"Don't worry, my love. You will soon."

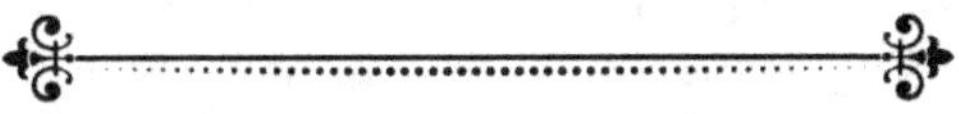

CHAPTER TWELVE

T HE INTRICACIES OF getting Penelope into his apartment at
The Grafton occurred to Yule only when the carriage pulled
up in front of the three-story brick residence. Yule's past amorous
encounters had always been undertaken in the lady's house, if she
were a widow, or at a discrete inn outside of London is she was
not. Never had he attempted to smuggle a lady into his own digs.
The Grafton, while not nearly as strict in its rules about such
goings on as the Albany, would definitely frown on such illicit
doings. So getting his betrothed into the structure, sight unseen,
might take more ingenuity than Yule had counted on. He sat
pondering the situation, wondering what repercussions would
descend upon him if they were caught going inside.

"What's wrong, Yule?" Penelope leaned forward, gazing out
at the tall building. "We do need to hurry a bit if we're to be back
home before Mama and Papa return."

"Well, the problem is, my dear, that ladies are not allowed
into gentlemen's digs. If you're caught going in—" He rolled his
eyes, thinking of the scandal that might incur. "—I could be
tossed out on my ear, with no recourse whatsoever."

She cocked her head. "We won't be living here when we're
married, will we?"

Yule shook his head. "No, I'll ask Grandfather if he has a small
estate we can take for the time being." If all of his cousins did

their parts and married by next August, he'd own the property outright as his spoils for the ongoing marriage wager.

She flashed him a grin. "Then what does it matter if they put you out? You'll be leaving shortly any way."

Taken aback by her unfailing logic, Yule had to chuckle. He'd not thought of that. Leave it to his cunning wife-to-be. "And so I will. Very well." He opened the door, still glancing around to see if anyone noted them. "Let us go in quickly. We don't want your reputation ruined regardless."

Penelope jumped down from the carriage and took his arm. "Lead on, MacDuff."

Yule bit back a sigh. Macbeth was such an ill-omened play. To evoke its ghost did not seem wise at the least. However, he dutifully led her up the sidewalk to The Grafton's entry, hurrying just a bit. No need to tempt Fate. At the door, he drew out his key and braced himself for the doorman's questions. Harrup couldn't forbid him entry to the building, although he would likely report that Yule had entered with a woman. Even though that woman was his fiancée, this was going to elicit talk.

Poking his head inside, Yule glanced around, ready for the onslaught of questions. Amazingly, the entry hall was empty. With the speed of a horse on Derby Day, Yule pulled Penelope inside and closed the door. He put his finger to his lips then tugged her toward the central marble staircase.

"Yes, my lord. I will have it summoned immediately." Harrup's voice exploded in the silence.

Yule clamped his fingers around Penelope's hand and took off up the staircase at a run.

The doorman had to be coming from one of the first-floor tenant's rooms, which gave them almost no time to climb to the second floor without being seen. Somehow Penelope kept stride with him and they turned the corner just as Harrup appeared calling, "Who is that?"

"Mr. Quartermain, Harrup," Yule called down, again motioning for Penelope to be quiet.

"Oh, very good, sir." The words drifted up as Harrup hurried outside, most likely to order a carriage for the first floor tenant.

"Come on." Yule heaved a sigh of relief as he took Penelope's hand and started up the stairs once more.

"How high up do you live?" she whispered.

"The third floor."

She nodded and they continued climbing until they stood at the next landing.

"This way." Yule led her down the left-hand corridor to the door at the far end on the right. "This is it. Number 309." He jangled the keys, looking for the correct one. His fingers were all thumbs now. Ah, at last. With one final look around, Yule turned the key in the lock and pushed the door open. A sudden noise at the end of the corridor had him pulling Penelope inside and into his arms.

She looked up at him, her smile widening. "I always knew you were a forceful one."

Yule groaned and stepped back.

"Good afternoon, sir." The muffled, low tones of his valet, Shaw, brought Yule to a halt. "You are back earlier than you anticipated."

Before the servant could put in an appearance, Yule thrust Penelope behind the screen meant to divide the room into both living and dining rooms.

"Yes, I did return sooner than I believed, Shaw." Yule allowed the man to help him off with his coat, furiously wondering whether he should confide in the valet or send him off on an errand that would keep him out of the flat for the next two or three hours. At last discretion won out. Shaw didn't need to know every bit of his business—at least not yet. This evening, when the man was cleaning up in the bedroom, he would likely require an explanation. "Miss St. Claire had a megrim, so I took her home. I'll call 'round there this evening to see if she's feeling better. Meanwhile, I believe I will nap for a while, so I won't require your services until I dress for dinner. Why don't you take the rest of the day? It is Boxing Day, after all. Consider an extra half-day as part of your present."

"Thank you, sir. That is kind of you." Shaw seemed genuinely touched. "Allow me to help you into your banyan."

Before Yule could protest, Shaw had him stripped naked and was slipping his blue silk robe over his shoulders. "There you are, Mr. Quartermain. Will there be anything else?"

Pulling the banyan around him and tying it firmly, Yule waved the valet away. "No, this is fine. Go enjoy yourself, Shaw. Merry Christmas."

The valet hurried into the dressing room with the clothing and Yule peeked around the screen, about to pull Penelope toward the bedroom, when he stopped, his jaw almost hitting his chest.

Penelope stood behind the screen where he'd left her, but not looking at all *as* he'd left her. Her gown, petticoats, and miraculously, her stays, were pooled in a puddle on the floor, leaving her standing in only her thin white linen shift. Her feet were still encased in clocked stockings, but her hair now swirled magnificently around her shoulders, released from the soft rolls around her face.

Yule's mouth dried, his heart beat frantically in his chest, and his cock sprang to attention so suddenly, it moved the folds of his banyan. Dear God, but she was the most beautiful creature he'd ever beheld. And if he didn't take her in his arms and sweep her into his bed this minute, he wouldn't have to hurry at all. He held out a hand to her, praying it didn't tremble. She put her hand in his and he drew her to him.

"God, Penelope. You are exquisite."

She gazed up at him, her smile making his chest constrict. "So are you, my love." She turned and led him toward the bed. "Now come, make me yours."

TREMBLING LIKE A leaf in a strong wind, Penelope didn't allow herself to stop until she and Yule stood before the tall poster bed that took up the middle of his bedroom. Much less confident about what they were doing than she'd let on to Yule, she still wished to go through with the plan. After all, she'd been waiting for this moment for most of her life—ever since she'd decided at the age of seven that she was going to marry Ulysses Quartermain. She hadn't known how or when, but she'd known with a surety that had sustained her through the long years since then that she would find him somehow and convince him to marry her.

And miracle of miracles, it had happened. They were going to be married—for all intents and purposes in the next half an hour, or however long it took to perform what Charlotte had told her was called carnal embrace. It didn't sound as earth-shattering as her sister had made it out to be. Perhaps it was something one had to experience in order to understand fully. And now she would experience it very, very soon. "Kiss me?"

Before her lips could form the word, Yule had sunk his mouth onto hers, sliding his tongue inside hers with the ease of breathing. Tingles shot down her arms and that peculiar feeling in the bottom of her stomach began to curl and tighten. Needing to feel him pressed against her body, Penelope slid her arms around his neck and pulled him to her. With their clothing so thin it might as well not be there, every muscle of his chest seemed to touch her from the top right down to the hard, prodding presence that pushed relentlessly against her nether regions. A low moan escaped her throat and suddenly she was swept up in Yule's arms and laid down in the middle of the big bed.

"Aren't we going to get under the covers?" This wasn't at all how she'd thought it would be.

"Later, my love." He climbed up in the bed beside her, looming large over top of her, his banyan more off him than on, so she could see his broad chest tapering down to his waist and lower—

"Oh, my." She could scarcely breathe when she beheld the

long, thick part of him that jutted toward her. Neither Charlotte nor Yule's sisters had described *that* in any of their whispered conversations. Probably with good reason. Frightened and thrilled at the same time, Penelope had to tear her gaze away and looked up at Yule, who was watching her carefully.

"Are you sure you want to do this, Penelope? Once it's done, it can't be undone." The tension in his voice and the dark, smoldering look in his eyes told of his willingness to continue this instant. Yet he held himself back, wanting to make certain of her.

Could there be a better, more caring man on God's green earth? "Yes, my love. We will be married in truth shortly and this is what married couples do, don't they?"

In answer he buried his face between her breasts, a low groan issuing from him as he answered, "Yes."

Penelope caught her breath as he suddenly enveloped her nipple in his mouth, disregarding the thin linen chemise that still covered her. Dear Lord! Her whole body heated instantly, including her cheeks that seemed suddenly aflame. As he sucked on the nipple, a streak of fire shot down to that strange place, low inside her and she gasped. To feel so good and so naughty at the same time was exhilarating.

A coolness rushed up her legs. Yule had pulled her chemise up, exposing the bottom half of her body. He raised up, shrugging off his robe. "Lift your bottom, sweetheart."

Startled, she did as he asked and he pulled her garment up and off her and tossed it over his shoulder, leaving her completely bare, exposed to his hungry gaze.

As he stared down at her, an appreciative growl came from low in his throat.

Somehow that made Penelope even more aware of her naked state, as no man had ever seen her before. She turned her head away, unwilling to meet his gaze anymore.

"Penelope." The coaxing tone in his voice made her turn back to him, though reluctantly. "You are beautiful, my love. Why do you turn away?"

She shrugged, unable to put her feelings into words.

"Here. Let me make you feel better." Yule settled down beside her, pulling her toward him until their bodies touched. He ran his hand down the length of her side, then her leg. As he began the journey back, he moved his hand between her legs, gently pushing them apart. "Relax, love. This won't hurt."

Penelope hadn't realized she'd been pressing her legs closed at his touch. Why was she acting so skittishly? She'd wanted this—wanted him—her whole life. There was nothing to be frightened of. Slowly, she loosened her legs, allowing his hand to glide between them all the way up to—

She gasped as he brushed the curls that covered her sex, shuddering as the new sensation overtook her.

"Shhh. It's all right."

His soothing voice helped allay her fears. This was Yule, the man she loved. If there was anyone she trusted, it was him. and she relaxed back into the mattress.

"Close your eyes and let me pleasure you."

Dutifully, Penelope closed her eyes and waited. When his fingers stroked through the curls this time, she didn't gasp, although she couldn't help trembling. This time, however, his finger touched a spot that made her cry out, not with pain but with intense pleasure.

"Did I hurt you?" Yule's voice was concerned, but she shook her head and opened her eyes to look up at him.

"No, it didn't hurt but..." How could she explain what she felt when he touched her like that?

"It felt good?" He caressed her there again in a small circular motion.

Oh, God. The sensation was like nothing she'd ever experienced before, as though her whole body was pulsing stronger and stronger until she moaned, "Yes."

Yule smiled broadly and continued the motion until Penelope was writhing with each delicious stroke. The strange sensation low in her belly coiled tighter and tighter until her hips rose of their own accord against his hand, seeking something...more. He swirled his finger over the little nub faster until Penelope shrieked as she shattered into wave after wave of a pleasure so deep, she never wanted it to end. Slowly, however, the sweet sensations began to subside and she slumped into the mattress, her head pillowed against Yule's shoulder.

A few moments later she looked up and beamed at him. "We're as good as married now, aren't we?"

A wry smile flickered over his face. "Not exactly, sweetheart."

She puckered her brow. Surely what just happened had been what Charlotte told her about.

Yule slid his arm from beneath her and pushed her legs open wider. "I'm afraid there is more to it, love. To be truly as one, I have to enter your body. Didn't they tell you that? That it would hurt?"

Oh, yes. Charlotte had said Phaedra mentioned there would be pain. Iphigenia said it was agony, but Penelope hadn't believed that. Now, looking at Yule rising over her, his...member looking larger and harder than before, she wasn't so sure his sisters weren't telling the truth. She nodded and attempted to put on a brave face. "They did say that."

Yule leaned down and kissed her, his tongue darting into her mouth as he shifted his body over hers.

She loved his kisses, and this one filled her with excitement again.

He broke the kiss and suddenly, between her legs, something large and hot pressed against her most intimate place. "I'll be quick and perhaps the pain will be less."

"Perhaps?" Penelope scarcely got the word out before Yule thrust forward. There was one agonizing pinch of pain, then he flowed into her, filling her up until he could go no further. Panting, Penelope narrowed her eyes, waiting for the pain to increase.

"Does it still hurt, love?" Yule gazed down at her, frowning.

"Not now." She glanced up at him. "Will it get worse?"

He grinned down at her. "No. It will only get better." With a little grunt, he pulled himself out, then slid carefully back in. "How is that?"

"It doesn't hurt." But she did feel awfully peculiar, so full and stretched.

"And it won't ever hurt again." Once more Yule withdrew and thrust back, a look of vast contentment on his face. "Penelope, my love. You feel so…good." He continued the rhythm, like waves crashing onto a shore and retreating, on and on until the circling sensation inside her awoke again. And with it a hunger for that final pleasure to come.

"Oh, Yule." She lifted her hips like before, seeking to meet his now frantic thrusts. Again and again, she rose toward him, until at last she shrieked as her body exploded around him, hugging his member. He strained against her, arching his back and crying out her name at the top of his voice. Moments later he sagged against her, his full weight bearing down on her.

Sweaty, but oh so pleased, Penelope put her arms around him. "And that was carnal embrace?"

With a groan, Yule rolled off her, breathing heavily. He flung an arm up over his face and nodded. "Yes, that was very definitely carnal embrace."

Grinning widely, Penelope snuggled against his side. "Good. Because if that wasn't it, I was going to change my mind about the whole thing."

"Too late for that now, my love." He gathered her to him. "You are mine and no other's for all time."

"That sounds so wonderful." Dreams actually did come true after all. "Now all we need to do is tell my parents what we've done and we'll be able to be married properly." That couldn't come too quickly for her.

Yule paused, then frowned. "Let me go to the Archbishop of Canterbury's offices first thing tomorrow and secure the special license. Then when your father tries to kill me for ruining you, I can show him that I am emphatically willing to marry you immediately."

Penelope sat up in the bed, eyes wide. She'd never considered that might happen. "You think Papa will try to kill you?"

"Well he won't call me out—that's not done any more—but I suspect he still might try to shoot me, if he's got a pistol handy." Yule's face had sobered. "Technically, you are ruined, my love."

"But only if we don't marry." She stretched out, luxuriating in the new closeness she now felt for him. He was her husband in all but name. "And we are getting married as soon as possible."

"I will be on the Archbishop's doorstep tomorrow morning at eight o'clock, then I'll come directly to you and we can speak to your parents." He pulled her over until she lay atop his naked body. "In the meantime, since the pantomime isn't due to end for another two hours, I thought we might enact our own panto-mime right here." He pulled her down for a searing kiss.

"What pantomime would that be, sir?" She giggled, loving this new, playful side to Yule.

"*The Lovesick Knight*," he said, flipping her onto her back and raising himself over her, "*or Harlequin Ravishes the Lady Fair.*"

"Ooh, I think I will enjoy that one more than *Robinson Cru-soe.*" Penelope slipped her arms around his neck and wrapped her legs around his hips.

Yule grinned as he slid into her once more. "I think I will too."

CHAPTER THIRTEEN

NEXT MORNING, AT precisely eight o'clock as promised, Yule's carriage pulled up at Morton's Tower, the entrance to Lambeth Palace, the residence of John Bird Sumner, current Archbishop of Canterbury. The imposing structure had been the entry to the Archbishop for some six hundred years and the worn, brownish-grey door he knocked on showed every single day of it. After plying the heavy metal knocker, Yule stood for several minutes looking around and up at the towering red-brick building, waiting for someone to come let him in. When no one appeared, he knocked again, this time louder and with more impatience.

All he wished to do was procure the special license, return to the St. Claire townhouse, confess yesterday's encounter with Penelope, then whisk her off to the nearest church with a vicar who'd agree to marry them. Ever since he'd made love to Penelope, the second time even more intensely satisfying than the first, he'd lived with no other thought save that he had to marry her as quickly as possible so he could keep her in his bed for at least a week, pausing their amorous activities only long enough to take in sustenance and an occasional nap.

But he could do none of that if the blasted clerk didn't answer the bloody door.

At last a creak, sounding like an ancient crypt being opened, alerted Yule that someone had finally realized that he was there. The door opened, revealing a harried looking clerk with huge dark smudges under his eyes.

"Good morning. I am Mr. Ulysses Quartermain and I wish to request an audience with the Archbishop." Yule had, via a hasty note to his grandfather last evening, obtained the correct protocol for applying for an audience with the Archbishop—and afterward how to apply for the special license itself. He had trusted his grandfather knew everything and once again, he was not disappointed.

"Good morning, Mr. Quartermain. I am sorry to be the bearer of bad tidings, however the Archbishop is ill this morning." The clerk looked saddened, whether because he'd disappointed Yule, was anxious for his employer, or was simply exhausted. "His physician is with him now, but I suspect the Archbishop will not be holding audiences for a week if not longer."

Yule's face must have turned a ghastly shade of white at that news, for he could feel the blood leaving his face in a rush that left him giddy. That couldn't be true. "Not for a week?"

"Or longer, sir." The clerk nodded mournfully. "I've seen the Archbishop with this malady before. He'll not stir one step for four or five days at the very least. He's always particular about his health."

"But...but what are people to do who need a special license to be married?" That was Yule's burning question now.

"They'd need to have the banns read or get a common license. Excuse me, sir, but I must attend His Grace." The clerk shut the door and Yule turned away, perplexed.

After yesterday's activities, he suspected he and Penelope needed to marry immediately. If they waited even for the reading of the banns, which took three weeks, and married on the third Sunday, people would still notice if their child came early. They would be perfectly capable of counting backward and finding a month lacking in the child's conception. There was no guarantee Penelope was now carrying his child, but Fate had a way of dealing people a losing hand just when they were least expecting it.

Of course, they could board a train and head for Scotland's Gretna Green, but even that desperate measure had been rendered almost moot by a little-known law, according to his cousin. Sandy had only been able to marry immediately in Scotland because he was a resident of a parish there. Those who were not had to wait several weeks before a wedding could be performed. So he might as well wait it out here. At least Penelope's parents might be better willing to overlook their little indiscretion if promised the large wedding Mrs. St. Claire had hoped for. It would simply be six months earlier than planned.

Still, he must persuade Penelope to keep their secret a little longer. It would do no good to worry her parents when nothing could be done about hurrying the wedding along. He'd continue to check at Lambeth Palace every morning and inquire about the Archbishop's health. With luck, they might be able to marry by the end of the week. Yule climbed back into his carriage and gave the St. Claires' address. He was looking forward to this conversation with Penelope about as much as he would a visit to an undertaker.

"YULE, WHAT A pleasant surprise so early in the morning." Mrs. St. Claire beamed at him as he entered the breakfast room. "James, lay another plate for Mr. Quartermain. How is your dear mother? Has she quite recovered from the exhaustion of the Christmas and Boxing Day festivities?"

"As well as can be expected, ma'am. The townhouse does belong to my grandparents, so Mother has few duties. But I will tell her you asked after her." If these pleasantries didn't come to an end immediately and Penelope didn't appear forthwith, he might go stark raving mad. "Has Penelope already breakfasted?"

"No, she has been a slug-a-bed all morning. Let me send for her. James—" Mrs. St. Claire sipped her coffee and shot a summoning look at the unwary footman. "Ask Brown to finish dressing Miss Penelope and send her down here immediately. She has lazed about too much this morning." She smiled at Yule. "Do sit down to breakfast with me. Mr. St. Claire finished half an hour ago and neither of the girls have put in an appearance."

"Thank you, ma'am." Yule slid into the chair opposite his hostess and another footman darted forward with a warm plate filled with eggs, ham, kippers, a slab of beef, and rolls with orange marmalade. Well, he probably needed a hearty breakfast, considering the task ahead of him. He dropped a napkin in his lap and speared a piece of ham. "Have you given any more thought to shortening the betrothal period?"

Mrs. St. Claire's coffee cup rattled in its saucer as the good lady's mouth opened in protest. "Of course not, Yule. What a thing to say." She eyed him suspiciously. "Why would you even think such a thing?"

"Well..." Yule forked up some of the eggs, put them in his mouth and chewed thoughtfully. He'd been feverishly thinking of reasons for him and Penelope to marry sooner rather than later— the most pressing one from yesterday's encounter at his flat being the last one he wished to mention despite what Penelope had said—and had hit on one he hoped might persuade his future mother-in-law to reconsider. "It's just that yesterday, when Penelope had that dreadful headache, I began to fear for her health. She's always seemed to be very well indeed, but now I'm not so certain." He looked meaningfully at Mrs. St. Claire. "She did have scarlet fever when she was a child, as I remember. The same time that Victor did."

He turned his concerned gaze on the woman, whose cheerful countenance suddenly drained of color. "I want her to have all the trappings of a long engagement, but not at the expense of damaging her constitution. It must be very taxing, attending all the parties as the guest of honor, being under the *ton*'s scrutiny for so many months. Seeing what a simple outing to the theater brought on, I am worried her health may go into a decline."

"Dear Lord!" Mrs. St. Claire dropped her roll back onto her plate untouched. "Do you think she may have come down with that horrible disease again? Her constitution was never the same afterwards, although as she grew up, she seemed to get stronger. Might that be why she hasn't appeared this morning? Oh, why has Brown not informed me that she is still ill?" She signaled a footman who hurried over. "Ask Brown to come to me in my room. I am going there this instant."

Yule saw a glimmer of hope at last, although he hoped he hadn't overplayed his hand.

"I was thinking perhaps a shorter engagement time, such as the three weeks it would take for the banns to be read, might limit the strain Penelope would be under." Given he couldn't obtain a special license for at least one week, another two weeks seemed almost tolerable. Of course, he'd burn in agony until he could be with her again the way they'd been yesterday, but he suspected they might find a way to devise another tryst or two while waiting for the wedding. And, in the event there was a child at the end of eight months instead of nine, the *ton*'s busybodies couldn't say much, as they'd have been married that whole long time. If they went into the country immediately after the wedding, who could say exactly when the child was born anyway.

Yule wasn't sure why he was so certain they had begotten a child yesterday, although it was probably merely a guilty conscience. "I wouldn't wish Penelope to suffer, or sink into dire distress because the wedding preparations proved too much for her."

"I must go and check on her. I won't leave this to Brown. If she is ill, she will need her mother." Rising hurriedly, Mrs. St. Claire dropped her napkin over her almost untasted plate. "There may be something to what you say, Yule." Mrs. St. Claire's face was now deeply drawn with worry. "I haven't given her illness a thought recently, because it was so long ago. But she's always been delicate, you know. After that dreadful fever… She hasn't had one of her headaches in ever so long, so I do wonder if the excitement of the betrothal and wedding aren't taking a toll on her."

"I wouldn't be at all surprised." Yule tried to keep the glee out of his voice. He truly didn't wish to worry Penelope's mother, but… "I see no harm in moving the wedding up. Then afterward Penelope and I could retire to grandfather's estate, away from the hubbub of London, where we would be close to you. There's nothing like the country for rest and recuperation."

"Oh, I must go to her, to make certain she'd not in a decline," Mrs. St. Claire said. "Thank you for pointing out how stressful this must be on her. Once we are certain of her health, I shall speak to Mr. St. Claire. Perhaps a shorter engagement period might be better for Penelope."

"Thank you, ma'am, for considering it." Yule kept his countenance serious, though inside he breathed a huge sigh of relief. "I'll wait to see how Penelope is and we can discuss what is best for her. If that's all right." Inspiration hit. "Why don't I take her for a carriage ride? Such an outing will certainly be good for her. There is nothing like fresh air to make one feel better."

"Thank you, my dear. I do appreciate you taking this in your stride." Her mother hurried out of the room and Yule turned back to his breakfast with renewed appetite.

About a quarter of an hour later, the door opened and Penelope entered, dressed in a charming deep pink gown frothy with lace, that almost took Yule's breath away. She was undeniably a beautiful woman, but there was something about her now, an added grace, a confidence, an ethereal glow that seemed to shout to him that she'd experienced the ultimate pleasure and been changed by it forever more. His heart swelled with pride at the thought that he'd been the one to bring about that change in her. He only hoped to God no one else saw it and realized it for what it was.

"Yule." Her face lit up when she spied him at the table, just finishing his coffee. "What on earth did you say to Mama? She's spent the last quarter of an hour feeling my forehead, patting my wrists, checking me all over for spots—which is most inconvenient when one is trying to dress—to see if I was coming down with a fever. I've not seen her so upset about my health since I had scarlet fever." Her eyes narrowed. "Did you have something to do with her now insisting on a three-week engagement instead of six months?"

"I fear I have, although I did not mean to worry her unduly." He motioned for her to sit and the footman brought her a plate. "I merely wished to make a case for a shorter engagement. Can you eat quickly? I've gotten permission to take you for a carriage ride."

"Oh, that sounds nice." She started in on the eggs and a piece of toast.

"I thought we would take a ride by some of the sights as we did yesterday." His gaze stayed on her until she looked at him. "When I brought you home."

Her eyes widened and her cheeks turned a bright pink. "I...I didn't think we'd be able to...to see those things again." They were both mindful of the listening servants. "So soon."

"I didn't either, but as I told your mother..." Yule stared deep into the widened blue eyes. "A carriage ride can do wonders for your health and well-being."

Galvanized, Penelope swallowed another mouthful of eggs and toast, took a bite of ham, and tossed her napkin down. "I must change, but I'll be down directly."

STANDING NAKED IN front of the roaring fire in Yule's bedroom, with him pressed against her from behind, cupping her breasts and kissing her neck, Penelope didn't think she could be happier than she was at this exact moment. Of course, she'd think that same thing as they made their way to the bed, when they were in the midst of carnal embrace, and during the long, lazy interlude afterward. Every moment they spent together in one another's arms was indescribably precious, undeniably erotic. She wanted to stay with him in this room, doing these incredibly pleasurable things forever.

Yule squeezed her nipples between his fingers, hardening them instantly and making Penelope moan and grind her backside into his groin. "Does that feel good, love?"

She nodded, loving the touch of his body everywhere on her. "It does. But I want more, Yule." Penelope pushed her bottom against his already hard member. "I want you."

He groaned into the neck, then nipped it lightly with his teeth. "Your wish is mine, sweetheart."

She arched her back, resting her head briefly on his shoulder, then turned toward the bed.

However, he caught her, pulled her back to him. "What if we did something…different?"

That sounded thrilling. "Different how?"

"Come here." He led her over to the chair at the desk.

Excitement bubbled up in her.

"Rest your hands on the chair seat."

Trembling with excitement, Penelope bent over and did so, spreading her hands over the leather cover. "Like this?"

"Exactly." Yule stood behind her, his cock—he'd told her yesterday that's what it was called—bumping against her. "Now spread your legs just enough…" He helped her position herself, his hands brushing against her nether regions and making her ache inside. Oh, but she loved doing this with Yule. Leaning over her back, he whispered into her ear, "I'm going to go deep into your body, love, much deeper than last night. I'll go slow but tell me if it's uncomfortable for you. If not, I think you'll enjoy it very much."

Now quivering with anticipation, Penelope gasped as Yule's hot hardness brushed against her opening. He nudged inside, then inched forward, filling her slowly, relentlessly until at last he'd seated himself completely within her. The sensation of fullness was more intense than yesterday, but not unpleasant. No, not unpleasant at all.

"How does that feel, love?" There was tension in Yule's deepened voice.

"Good." The word came out huskier than normal. "Very good."

"Then I'll start." Yule rocked back slowly, withdrawing almost all the way, then sinking himself all the way back inside her.

The sensation of him sliding so far inside her, filling her so full she thought she might burst, brought the deep-down ache at her core to life once more. "Ummm."

"Did that hurt?"

"No, it feels incredibly good." Nothing had ever felt so wonderful. "Don't stop."

"I won't." He pulled back and thrust forward again, a little faster this time. "How's that?"

"Oh, God, wonderful." The ache inside was beginning to spiral, closer and closer with every thrust. Yule's movements reached a steady rhythm, neither fast nor slow, but enough to keep her winding slowly toward that ultimate explosion.

"I'm going to touch you now, sweetheart." Even as he spoke, Yule's hand slid beneath them, again brushing the sensitive little nub above her opening.

"Ahh." The immediate jolt made her shudder, although she didn't tip over into the ultimate pleasure. Lord, she was close though. Her body seemed to hum with energy that was working toward a release of monumental proportions.

Yule stroked deeply, his cock pounding into her, bringing her closer and closer to the edge. Then his fingers pressed firmly on her nub and her body convulsed around him.

Penelope threw back her head, crying out his name as wave upon wave of immeasurable pleasure crashed over her. Her body danced to its own rhythm now, although Yule still pumped into her, once, twice more until he bellowed her name and strained against her, his hot essence pouring forth deep inside her.

Panting together, Yule leaned against her as Penelope's legs threatened to buckle. She let the chair hold them both up until Yule guided them to the bed, lifted her into it, then followed after. They crawled under the covers and snuggled together. Penelope was so completely sated, she could scarcely keep her eyes open.

Still one question nagged at her. "Yule?"

"Hmm?" He sounded asleep as well.

"You told me the Archbishop is ill and can't issue a special license for at least a week. So we can't get married immediately. Yet you wanted us to make love again today and often, you said, until we are married." She cocked an eyebrow at him. "Isn't that dangerous?"

Her question had roused him, and he settled himself with one arm behind his head. "It would be most dangerous if we were not going to be married until June as your mother originally decreed. However, as she is now considering moving the wedding up to three weeks from the time the first banns were read, which was last Sunday—" He leaned over and kissed her soundly on the lips. "—I realized if you are now carrying our child, I don't care what the *ton* thinks about the baby coming early. What matters is that we can love one another as much as we wish, as often as we can. So the busybodies can go hang." He pulled Penelope to him and wrapped his arms around her. "You are the most important thing in my life now, sweetheart. Nothing can take you away from me."

"Or you from me." Penelope snuggled closer to him. "'Til death do us part."

CHAPTER FOURTEEN

January 8, 1861
Hertfordshire, England

"You mustn't overtire yourself, Penelope. You've only got one more week to prepare for the wedding. You must save your strength." Mama sipped her tea to fortify her as they sat in the drawing room, going over the list of things still left to do for the big event. She'd been atwitter with advice about Penelope's health ever since Yule had reminded her mother that Penelope's constitution might not be very strong. It was a boon as far as the wedding was concerned, however it was maddening not to be able to do any of the most pleasant pastimes the countryside could offer in winter, such as skating and sleigh rides.

The monotony would be endurable if Yule was with her, but that decision had been taken out of their hands. On the eve of their departure to their home estate in Hertfordshire, just after they'd rung in the New Year, Yule had been commanded to remain in London at his grandfather's request regarding some family business.

Ever since they'd arrived at Clairemont, Penelope had mourned the loss of London and even more the loss of Yule's constant companionship. They'd become quite adept that last week at creating outings in the afternoons to mask their amorous trysts at his rooms. Now she'd been without him for four whole days and her body ached to feel his arms wrapped around her once more as he plunged into her, making her world shatter around her.

"I will be careful, Mama." Not that she needed to be. Truth be told, she'd not been allowed to do a single thing ever since her wedding had been hastily moved up. Mama was so afraid she'd tire herself out, either she, Charlotte, or a footman did everything for her. It gave her a new understanding of the phrase "being waited on hand and foot."

Her enforced idleness, however, had given her lots of time to think about various topics, one of which was what the ladies of the *ton* had made of the drastic change in the date for the wedding. Quite likely, they'd surmised Penelope was in a family way, which might indeed be true, although Penelope had no clue if she was. Still, the busybodies who kept track of such things had likely been waiting for her to swoon in public or begin to remain sequestered at home awaiting the little bundle of joy. Now that she was no longer in London for them to speculate about, she supposed they would fasten their attention on the next innocent victim. Penelope sighed. In some ways, she was glad to be out of the city. "Although there's nothing particularly dangerous or diverting in Hertfordshire for me to be careful about."

"I am not too certain of that, my dear." Mama leaned toward her, a twinkle in her eye. "I received a note this morning from Lady Elizabeth Weston. She is coming for tea this afternoon to welcome us back to the neighborhood on behalf of the Quartermain family."

"That is terribly nice of her." Most likely that call had been precipitated by her engagement to Yule, although the duke's family at Welwyn Castle had always been friendly with them, of course.

"She's bringing her eldest son with her." Now Mama was almost beside herself with the excitement of this news. "Mr. Thomas Weston, you may recall. You danced with him at the

Kastners' party."

"Tom Weston!" That took Penelope aback. She remembered her encounter with Tom perfectly well. He'd wanted to make Yule jealous of his dancing with her and had succeeded royally. "Oh, yes, I do remember him. Yule tells me he's quite the rake now he's captain of his own ship."

"And quite an eligible bachelor as well." Mama sipped her tea innocently.

"Well, I am spoken for, thank you very much." Penelope raised her nose. Tom had been exciting, but much too wild for her. She'd considered him husband material for the briefest of seconds when trying to get Yule to notice her, but she'd never been serious about setting her cap for him.

"You are not the only eligible young lady in this house, Miss Penelope. Your sister could do worse than bringing Mr. Weston up to scratch." The lace on Mama's cap threatened to fly off she nodded her head so vehemently.

"I'm not so certain—"

"Lady Elizabeth Weston and Mr. Thomas Weston, ma'am."

Penelope sat up quickly, a pleasant smile on her face. She'd have to remind Mama about certain aspects of Tom Weston's outrageous behavior, which her mother had conveniently forgotten. If she thought she'd be able to make a match between Charlotte and Tom, Mama was surely building an elaborate castle in the air.

"Lady Elizabeth, Mr. Weston." Mama had on her most pleasant smile. "So very nice to see you. Lady Elizabeth this is my youngest daughter, Penelope. She is to marry Mr. Ulysses Quartermain, as I'm sure you know. And you are already acquainted with her, Mr. Weston?"

"Tom and I are good friends, aren't we, Tom?" Penelope intended to take the upper hand with Tom during the tea, so hopefully things would not get out of hand.

"Very good friends, Penelope, although I understand you have completely thrown me over for Yule now." Grinning, Tom helped himself to a cup of tea, dropped in an amazing four lumps of sugar, gave the cup as quick stir, and sat promptly beside her on the sofa.

"That should be no surprise to you. When we met, I was hoping to become much better acquainted with Yule." She grinned back at him. "As you may have heard, that has happened."

"I do hear you should be wished happy. May I kiss the bride?" He waggled his eyebrows at her salaciously and Penelope laughed merrily at his antics. No woman could ever hope to tame this Quartermain cousin.

"On the cheek as a proper cousin should." She presented it and he barely grazed it with his lips.

He eyed her boldly as he sipped his tea. "I suppose I shall have to hope for better things when you throw Yule over and marry me instead." The vibrant energy that emanated from Tom was infectious. "I am confident I can bring you around eventually."

"I would not hold my breath in anticipation of that, sir." Penelope chuckled. She had to admit, Tom was fun to talk to and flirt with as long as she didn't let it go too far.

"So you have no objection to becoming one of the Welwyn wager brides?" Tom held out his cup and Mama poured more tea into it.

"What is a wager bride?" Penelope frowned and cocked her head. She'd never heard of that term for a bride.

"You know, the wager all of us cousins are participating in." Tom grabbed a finger-sized cucumber sandwich and ate it in one bite. "Yule told you about it, didn't he?'

No, he hadn't. And now Penelope had to wonder why. "I don't remember what he said. Why don't you tell me?"

"Well, Grandfather wagered with the six of us cousins of marriageable age that we couldn't marry within the year." Tom reached for another sandwich. "If we do, all of us win an estate, carriages, and ten thousand pounds." He cocked his head. "Yule didn't tell you any of this?"

"I daresay he did, but I may not have been paying attention." That was a baldfaced lie, but Penelope needed to know more about this wager. "What happens if you don't all marry?"

"Oh, well then none of us gets a thing and the others will have married for nothing." About to take a sip of tea, Tom froze over his teacup. "Not actually for nothing, I assume. They would have married a woman they cared for at least. Or I'd hope they'd done so."

"Have many of you married so far?" Penelope had to keep her question short as it was becoming difficult to speak.

"Only Alex and Sandy." He grinned at her. "The rest of us are taking our time. But you and Yule are next, it seems."

"Had your two cousins known their wives long before they married?" How had Yule not told her any of this? Suspicions were rising, but she tried to beat them down.

"Not at all." Tom gave her a smirk. "Alex met Emma at a weekend house party and married her at the end of it. And Sandy met his bride at a ball in September and they were married in October. So Yule will be the first one to have known his bride for more than a month before the wedding." Tom chuckled and reached for a seed cake. "I will tell you, I'm certain he was relieved when you turned up at the Kastners' house party. Before that, he hadn't a clue who he was going to marry. Said he might give me a run for last place in the marriage race."

That made all too much sense to Penelope. When she and Yule had first met at the Kastners' party, he'd been extremely standoffish toward her. In fact, he'd been so resistant, she'd had to pursue him until he'd finally given in. And once they'd agreed to marry, he suddenly hadn't wanted to wait. It was as if he *couldn't* wait six months to marry her. Had that been why he'd been so eager to bed her? If he got her with child, she'd have no choice but to marry him, neatly fulfilling his part of the marriage wager.

Gritting her teeth in an effort to keep her tears from flowing, Penelope mumbled an "Excuse me," then rose and ran from the room, her budding suspicions all but confirmed. She'd managed to become betrothed to the one man she loved with all her heart and soul, only to discover all along he'd just needed a bride—and any bride would have done.

"THIS JUST CAME for you, Mr. Quartermain." His grandfather's butler handed Yule an envelope as he sat with the afternoon paper in the drawing room. The address was scribbled in a hand so illegible, he could scarcely make out his own name. There was no return address, however the letter had been posted from Hertfordshire, so he surmised it had come from Penelope. Eagerly, he tore into the envelope.

He'd been detained in Town conferring with his grandfather about leasing a suitable estate in Hertfordshire for him to bring his bride to, near enough to both their families' estates that he and Penelope could continue to cherish their society while enjoying the privacy necessary for newlyweds. Yule had informed his grandfather that if the wager went as scheduled, he'd like the estate—Mulberry Park—to be part of his share of the winnings. If not, he'd buy it from his grandfather if Penelope approved of it.

Yule pulled the letter out and flicked it open, frowning immediately. The handwriting was unmistakably that of a gentleman, though it was as illegible as the envelope's direction. A glance at the signature had him shaking his head. "Tom? What the devil is Tom doing up in Hertfordshire?"

He read the missive, but two sentences in, Yule leaped to his feet. What the devil was going on at home? He glanced at the letter again, hoping to find the words different somehow, but they unfortunately remained the same.

Dear Cuz,

You'd better pop up here to calm down your bride-to-be. She's gotten into a tizzy about the marriage wager for some reason, and now may not be willing to marry you anymore. Will see you when you arrive.

Yours,
Tom

What in blazes had his cousin said to Penelope…wait. He reread the letter again and uttered a vile curse. Tom had spoken to her about the *marriage wager*. And that had made her wish to change her mind about marrying him? As if she could do that now that they'd thrown caution to the wind and become lovers. Very active lovers too. Currently, Penelope possessed knowledge of the marriage bed some ladies didn't discover until after they'd borne children.

"Tate!" Yule bellowed for the butler. There was nothing for it but to head to Hertfordshire as soon as possible to find out what mischief his cousin had stirred up this time. "Send a footman to King's Cross to see when the next train to Welwyn leaves."

"Very good, Mr. Quartermain." Tate assessed the situation perfectly, and inquired, "Shall I inform your valet of your departure?"

"Yes, thank you, Tate." Much as he wished he could strangle Tom for telling him so little, he feared he'd need his cousin's assistance in straightening out whatever he'd said to offend Penelope. What could he have said about the wager that would have set her off so? He'd told Penelope about the marriage wager, hadn't he? Try though he might, he couldn't remember. He'd stop at the telegraph office on the way to the station and let Tom know when to send the carriage for him. What an utter mess. Yule stormed upstairs to change, each step feeding his anger.

Shaw was already packing his valise when Yule burst into his room. "I took the liberty of packing only the necessities for tonight and the next couple of days, Mr. Quartermain. When will you know if you will be remaining in Hertfordshire?"

"I have no bloody idea, Shaw." Yule stood impatiently as the man stripped him then re-dressed him in a suit of serviceable dark blue for the grimy ride to come. "I have no clue what trouble my cousin has landed me in, or even if it's a true crisis or simply a storm in a teacup. I won't know until I arrive at Grandfather's."

"I do hope it is the latter, sir." Shaw brushed the shoulders of the jacket and straightened it for good measure. "There you are sir. I'll have your valise downstairs as soon as I've finished packing. What train are we to leave on?"

"I'm waiting for word from the footman. There used to be a five-forty that arrived in Welwyn at half-past seven, but I've not kept a check on the times of late, since Grandfather's moved to London almost permanently.

"I'll have everything ready, sir." The valet gathered up the discarded clothing and commenced shaking them out and laying them neatly on the bed.

"Good man, Shaw." Glancing once in the mirror to make certain he didn't have the air of a lunatic, Yule set his mouth into a firm, rather than grim, line and left.

Shaw was as good as his word. Before the footman had returned with the next three departures of the train from King's Cross station, the valet had the packed valise in the entry hall, and Yule's overcoat, hat, and stick at the ready. Tate summoned the carriage and Yule departed like an efficient clockwork machine. He only hoped the entire trip and especially its conclusion would continue as well as the beginning.

TRUE TO HIS word, Tom had the carriage waiting when Yule's train finally pulled into the station, despite the fact he was more than three hours late. There had been trouble with the engine when they arrived at Harlow and a new one had to be procured. Yule had been certain they would shut down the train completely, causing him to have to stay the night there. However, miracle of miracles, a new engine was acquired and installed, delaying them for a matter of hours instead of days. Yule had ground his teeth the whole time, wishing for a stiff brandy.

When Yule opened the carriage door, he was surprised to see Tom there. The man had guts, he had to say, considering the choice words he'd sent him via telegraph.

"Just calm down, Yule." Tom sat in the backward facing seat, a sure sign of contrition on his part. "Nothing's been said about calling off the wedding, except by Penelope. Her parents are still sure she can be calmed down." His cousin's face took on a perturbed look. "Why in hell didn't you tell her about the wager? Are you truly daft?"

"You've got some nerve to blame me for what was obviously your fault, Tom. Why were you speaking about the wager anyway? Why the devil are you even in Hertfordshire?"

"All I did was accompany Mother here at Grandfather's request. Since he and Grandmama were remaining in London, he sent us as the welcoming delegation for the St. Claires. So we called there for tea. I hadn't seen Penelope since the Kastners' party and wanted to catch up with her, especially to hear about the upcoming wedding plans." Tom's eyes narrowed and his glare increased. "Of course, I'd mention the marriage wager. It's the reason you're marrying, isn't it?"

"Absolutely not." How dense could his cousin be? "I'm marrying her because I love her."

"And how was I to know you were keeping the wager a secret from her? A singularly stupid decision on your part, I must say."

"I was being stupid?" Yule couldn't believe his cousin's gall. "I didn't tell Penelope about the wager because in the beginning, I didn't want her to know I was looking for a wife. I thought it would make her pursue me even more strenuously. Then, after I fell in love with her, it didn't seem to matter because I *wanted* to marry her and the date of the wedding wouldn't impact the wager in any case. So to me, it didn't matter. But now you've spilled the beans and I'm left having to explain something I never thought I needed to explain to her in the first place." Yule dropped his head into his hands as the carriage continued briskly out of town toward Welwyn Castle.

Tom shook his head. "I should have telegraphed back to you to bring the biggest damned diamond you could find as an appeasement to Penelope." He lit up a cigarette. "I've heard it is more difficult to jilt someone who's offering you a diamond. Perhaps there's a jeweler in Harlow we can run over to tomorrow before you go see Penelope."

"I am not going to bribe the woman into marrying me, Tom." Not that he thought something like jewels would sway Penelope the least bit once she made her mind up. "And I'm going to their house tonight. I've got to see Penelope, to make this right with her."

"It's close to midnight. I don't think it will do you any good to go in there and rouse everyone up from their beds. You'd be better to leave it until the morning."

Yule gazed out the window at the inky blackness of the countryside. When he could make out the shape of a house, it was invariably dark. Perhaps Tom had a point in waiting for daylight. "Very well, but first thing in the morning, I'm going over there."

"I wouldn't dream of standing in your way. But I will tell you, you'd better think up something to say before you go. You can't simply ask her to come back to you." Tom chuckled. "It'll be the shortest refusal of a proposal in the history of the world."

"I don't need to propose to her again. She's agreed to marry me. Several times." And in several different places—parlor, the bed, the bedroom chair, the bathtub in his dressing room. He might have proposed each time they climaxed together. However, if she was as upset as Tom seemed to think, he was going to have the devil's own time finding a way to get her back if she was now set on refusing him.

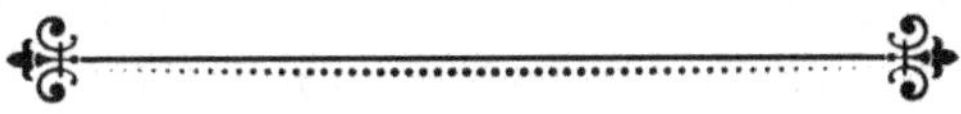

CHAPTER FIFTEEN

THE DAY HAD dawned cold and rainy, typical weather for January in Hertfordshire as Penelope looked out across the frozen lawn after another sleepless night. The wretchedness of the morning certainly fit her mood, grim and gray. Her face was still swollen from all the crying she'd done the past few days, her heart irreparably bruised by Yule's perfidy.

Never had she felt so absolutely stupid as when Tom had told her Yule was part of a wager in which he had to marry in order for him and his cousins to win. Yule's puzzling about-face behavior toward her now made sense. From the moment he'd met her at Mr. Kastner's house party, he'd made it clear that he wasn't interested in her. Yet she'd persisted, pestering him, trying to make him like her just because she'd had this silly *tendre* for him all the time she'd been growing up. Ever since he'd given her Mrs. Phillpotts.

She glanced over at the little rag doll, resting serenely on her pillow as she'd done ever since Yule had given her to her when she was seven. Now the poor thing was terribly bedraggled, with bits of her clothing missing and her mop cap permanently askew. Still, Penelope couldn't go to sleep at night unless Mrs. Phillpotts was clutched in her arms.

Dragging herself from the window over to the bed, she grabbed the rag doll and peered into her face. "He doesn't love me, Mrs. Phillpotts. I suspect now he never did. So I don't know why he gave you to me. I believed at the time it meant he liked me, that he cared about me at least a little." She tried to smooth down the turned-up hem of the doll's dress, but it refused to behave and curled right back up. "I was wrong about that. And I was wrong to think I could change his mind. He tried to tell me when we met again, but I refused to listen. I kept pushing him until he gave in and that persuaded me he loved me. Only he didn't." A single tear slipped from her eyes and trickled down her cheek, then dropped onto Mrs. Phillpott's endlessly serene porcelain face. "He just said those things so I'd marry him and win his wager for him."

The most galling part of it was that she'd still likely have to marry him. Oh, but he'd laid the trap all too cleverly. He'd seemed fine with the long engagement until they were finally engaged. Once that was done, he changed his tune and tried to persuade her that six months was too long a time to wait. And stupid girl that she was, she'd played right into his scheme. She'd been the one to hit upon how they could anticipate their wedding night and as soon as she had, her fate had been sealed.

Of course, she hadn't seen it that way at the time. She'd been thrilled to experience all the mysteries of the marriage bed while not actually being married. Because they were going to be married and live happily ever after because they loved one another. Or so she'd thought. But Yule had deceived her. He'd not been in love with her. If he had been, he'd have told her about this wretched wager and assured her that he was marrying her because he loved her, not because he needed to marry someone. Oh, no, she was only the convenient young lady who agreed to have him.

According to Tom, Yule had had no other prospects in the way of marriageable ladies. And who would blame them, if they knew he only wanted to marry because of the wager? He must have been afraid she'd hear of it and renege on marrying him. That was why he'd been mad to get the special license and when that wasn't possible, he'd managed to get her mother to agree to waiting only for the banns, which would be completed this coming Sunday. Well, it would be a cold day in hell when she married Ulysses Quartermain.

Unless she was now carrying his child.

"Penelope?"

She jumped at the unexpected sound of Charlotte's voice. "What is it?"

"Mama wanted to know if you were coming down to breakfast." As if she couldn't bear to look at Penelope, Charlotte stood outside the room, the door opened just a crack.

"I'm not hungry." She hadn't been able to eat much at all since that awful day.

"You must keep up your strength."

"What for?" Her life was probably over. Or if not, was going to be completely miserable if she had to marry a man who didn't love her. Given a choice, she'd rather starve to death.

The door opened wider and Charlotte stared at her, her eyes furtive. "Yule is downstairs asking for you."

Penelope's heart gave a huge leap as though it wanted to escape her chest and rush down the stairs of its own accord. She turned her back on Charlotte, so her sister couldn't see the longing that must be evident on her face. If she'd thought to persuade herself she didn't still care for Yule, her reaction to news of his presence said she was a fool. Despite how miserable she'd been for the past days, she did love him still.

So where did that leave her? Did she simply forgive him and move past his betrayal? Could she bring herself to marry a man who would wed her only to win a wager? Marriages had been made for less honorable reasons, she supposed. But did she wish hers to be one where she loved him desperately and he cared little for her?

He'd seemed to care very much when they were in bed together, giving each other incredible pleasures. She suspected he would continue to do so if they married. With no true feeling behind the act, however, would the pleasure continue to satisfy her? Or him?

Penelope drew in a hitching little sob. There was so much she needed to consider before she could see him again. "Tell him I am not well," she called to her sister. "He must come back tomorrow or the day after. I…I have to think of what to say to him."

"All right. If that's what you wish." Charlotte closed the door with a quiet click, leaving Penelope to the silence of the room.

At least that request would give her a little time to try to decide what she was going to do. Of course, as her parents didn't know she and Yule had been intimate—she could wait and see if anything untoward would come from their numerous couplings in carnal embrace. If there were no consequences, then she'd have more choices available to her. However, if she was with child, there would be no question but she would have to marry him. It might be best to wait then.

The sound of the front door slamming shut reverberated all the way up to her chamber. Yule had apparently gone, without entreating her further. The tiny hope that he would have sent Charlotte back to beg Penelope to come downstairs—perhaps signaling that he did care for her at least a little—extinguished abruptly, like a candle being snuffed.

Tears pricked her eyes, an anger such as she'd not felt in ages rolling over her. Her gaze fell on Mrs. Phillpotts, still clutched in her hand. A connection to Yule she'd treasured for years. No more. With an anguished cry, she flung the little rag doll into the fireplace. It landed squarely on the blazing flames and immediately began to smoke.

Stricken, Penelope jumped from the bed, ran to the fireplace, and snatched the doll back, beating out the flames that had caught on the disheveled clothing. Penelope hugged Mrs. Phillpotts to her, the smell of the scorched cloth acrid in her nostrils. She couldn't stand to think of having to go a single night without holding the doll in her arms. It was her one link to Yule all these years, to the memory of the boy who hadn't wanted her to be friendless. "Oh, Mrs. Phillpotts." She squeezed her eyes shut and held the doll close. "What am I going to do?"

One hour earlier

THE SUN HADN'T climbed too high in the sky the next morning before Yule and Tom had set out in the carriage for the St. Claires' home. Even though he was still angry at Tom for bringing this catastrophe down on him, Yule still wanted him there, not only for moral support, but so he could eventually apologize to Penelope for causing all the trouble. Once Yule could speak to her, he could explain and reassure her that the wager had nothing whatsoever to do with his desire to marry her.

Crisp snow made the carriage wheels crackle as they hurried toward the smaller estate nestled at the bottom of a hill—the manor house Yule remembered well from his childhood. Pale red brick trimmed in white, the structure didn't seem to have changed at all in ten years. Thick ivy grew in the front and curled around the side of the house, seeming to anchor the building to the ground. He'd played here with Victor and Penelope every chance he could. Funny he was coming back now, a gentleman every bit as uncertain as the boy had been fearless. Of course, then he hadn't been in love with Penelope.

The carriage pulled to a stop and Yule jumped down and strode to the front door.

"You know it's entirely too early to pay a call." Tom's voice sounded thin through the fierce wind that blew around the stoop and the semicircle made from the front rooms of the house.

"I suppose it is, but I'm not putting this visit off until later." Yule had passed a sleepless night, tossing and turning, worrying about his reception at the St. Claires' home. He assumed her parents still didn't know about his and Penelope's afternoon activities, the only good thing he could think of at the moment.

He dreaded having to tell the St. Claires why he must, at all costs, marry their youngest daughter. They would certainly not be happy, and neither would they blame Penelope in the slightest. Yule was older, he was the man, and of course he must have seduced her. Yule would be hard pressed to say who had actually seduced whom, although their first encounter had been planned and perpetrated by Penelope. He simply hoped it would not come to that.

"Well, at the least they should give us breakfast." Tom put on his most pleasant smile as the door was opened by Stokes, the St. Claires' long-time butler. Yule had known him as a boy. The butler must be ancient by now, a wizened little man who still stood straight and motioned both of them into the entry hall.

"Stokes, will you tell Miss Penelope I have come to call on her?" Yule tried to make it sound as if he often arrived to pay a call at seven-thirty in the morning.

"Yes, Mr. Quartermain. Will you come this way?" Unruffled, Stokes led them to a small receiving chamber. "Wait here, sirs." Without another word, Stokes turned on his heel and left.

"His tone did not bode well, old chap." Tom slapped Yule on the shoulder and grinned at him. "He sounds like the Grim Reaper himself."

"Stokes has always sounded like that. He's not improved in ten years either, I can tell you. The man always sounded like gloom and doom." Hopefully, it was simply his normal tone and the butler didn't have any particular knowledge of Penelope or her feelings toward him.

Yule paced up and down the tiny room, unable to even look at the paintings on the walls. They were all very tasteful, he was sure. But Mr. and Mrs. St. Claire weren't great connoisseurs of art, or so he'd heard his grandfather say. He doubted he was missing much—except Penelope.

"Do you think they will have kippers and sausages, Yule?" Tom looked up at him seriously. "I could eat an ocean of kippers and a whole hogshead of sausages."

"Well, don't try to eat them out of house and home. I'm trying to salvage my marriage and you're planning to settle in for the duration." Disgusted with his cousin, Yule turned his back on Tom and stalked over to the window that looked out on the snow-covered parkland.

"Moping about whether or not she's coming down isn't going to do either her or you much good." Tom was staring at the paintings, a puzzled look on his face. "I certainly wouldn't have paid for this monstrosity."

"Remind yourself whose house this is, Tom, and keep your opinions to yourself." Irked, Yule paced back and forth across the small room. He stared hard at his cousin, who seemed unconcerned at best.

Stokes popped his head back into the room. "This way if you please, sirs. Mr. and Mrs. St. Claire wish you to come to the large family drawing room." He led them down the corridor quite a long way, until they came to a very nicely furnished chamber, the walls done in a cool blue with white accents.

Mr. St. Claire, a short, lean gentleman greeted them with a smile. "Good morning, Yule. Good morning, Tom. I'm glad you've come. Penelope hasn't eaten, hasn't seen anyone, and has barely slept according to her maid. Do you know what it was that happened at tea the other day to upset her so?"

"I do, Mr. St. Claire." He turned to glare at Tom. "It was my cousin's talking out of turn that has brought this all on."

"All my wife has been able to get out of her is that you betrayed her, that you don't love her, and you only want to marry her to win a wager." The mild-mannered gentleman Yule had known years ago, turned steely eyes on him now. "Is that true? And if it is, how could you do such a thing to Penelope? And if it's not, what did *you* say—" He turned on Tom. "—to make her think it's true?"

With one searing glare at Tom, Yule launched into the tale, not sparing Tom's involvement in the least. "So that is how she came to doubt my true intentions toward her. Although I cannot believe she would think I wanted to marry her just to win a wager. She must know me better than that."

"She's always taken everything so much to heart, Yule." Mrs. St. Claire spoke up, dabbing her eyes with a handkerchief. "You may not remember it, but when Victor died, Penelope was inconsolable, sick as she was. Even worse, right on the heels of his death, we had to uproot her when we moved to Ireland. Back then, like now, she wouldn't eat, she wouldn't speak. She shut herself off from everything and everyone except—" She sent Yule a furtive glance. "Except for you. Because of that little doll you gave her the morning we left."

"Mrs. Phillpotts."

"You remember?" Mrs. St. Claire's brows rose. "After all these years?"

"I do." That morning had been etched into his memory, although he never understood why. Now perhaps he had an inkling.

"She loved that doll so much. Carried it everywhere. Wouldn't hear of tossing it out when she got to be a young lady." Her mother shook her head. "She still has it, Yule."

From above came a quiet step on the stairs that were out of sight. Mr. St. Claire nodded to the staircase. They all turned and looked upward.

Yule held his breath, hoping against hope he would see Penelope, but moments later, her sister Charlotte appeared. Her eyes widened when she saw Yule.

"Charlotte, dear," Mrs. St. Claire wiped a tear away and nodded to her other daughter. "Run back upstairs and tell Penelope Yule is here asking for her."

Looking as though she'd rather face a firing squad, Charlotte nodded and returned up the stairs.

Perhaps her sister could persuade her to come and at least talk to him. If he could just sit down with Penelope and explain what had happened, surely she would understand and agree once more to marry him. Wouldn't she?

Yule looked at Mr. and Mrs. St. Claire sitting there anxiously. Of course, there was another way. He could simply tell them he and Penelope had anticipated the wedding night. That was an understatement, of course, but just knowing they'd been intimate once would be enough for her father to insist Penelope marry him. The problem was, he didn't want to trap her into marriage that way. He wanted her to come to him because she loved him, as he loved her. Not because someone had forced her to do so. How had something so wonderful turned out so horribly in the blink of an eye?

"Yule."

Charlotte's voice interrupted his thoughts, and he looked up at her hopefully.

"Penelope says she is unwell. She needs time to think about what to say to you. She wants you to come back tomorrow." Charlotte kept her gaze on the floor. "Because she can't see you today."

Gritting his teeth so he wouldn't say something he knew he'd regret, Yule made an attempt at a bow toward the St. Claires, mumbled something between his clenched teeth, and headed for the door. Penelope was better than this. She'd always been fair in the past. Why wouldn't she give him the chance to explain?

Without waiting for Stokes to open the door, Yule pulled it open, strode over the threshold, and slammed it behind him, almost clipping Tom's elbow as the massive door hit the frame.

"Bad luck with that, old chap." Tom looked up at the lightening gray sky. "At least it stopped raining. That's a good omen, don't you think?"

Yule gave him a withering look and continued down the snow-covered path toward their waiting carriage.

His cousin raced after him. "Perhaps when we come back tomorrow, she'll have calmed down enough to see you. I know once you see her, she'll let you explain."

Yule stopped, one foot on the carriage's step. "About that I believe you're right, Tom." He sent a keen glance at his cousin and smiled for the first time that morning. Yule stepped back, almost bumping into Tom, then he struck off toward the right side of the manor house, leaving clear tracks in the slushy snow.

"Where the hell are we going, Yule?" Tom picked his way toward him, but Yule was through with waiting.

"I'm going to see Penelope now." Spurred on by his own words, he mumbled under his breath. "Whether she wants me to or not."

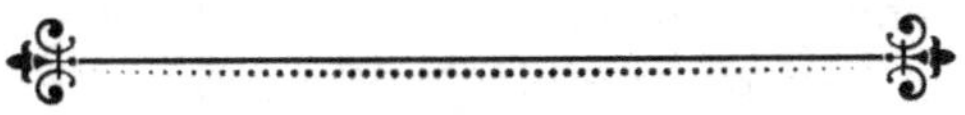

CHAPTER SIXTEEN

STRIDING AS FAST as he could, occasionally slipping in the snow, Yule headed around the side of the manor house to a section of vine-covered bricks he remembered well from his boyhood. He wrapped his hand around one of the ropes of thick creeper and gave a preparatory pull. He'd not done this for over a decade and he wanted to make certain the plant wasn't going to come away from the wall and land him on his back on the hard snow-covered ground.

"What the hell do you think you're doing?" Tom had finally caught up to him, glaring at him as though he were mad.

"I'm going to climb up there and talk with Penelope." He was certain if he could only talk to her, he could straighten this whole mess out.

"You're going to kill yourself. You realize that, don't you?" Tom tried to pull him away from the wall, but Yule shrugged him off.

"I'll do no such thing. I used to climb this wall almost every week when I was a boy." It had been one of the great joys and excitements of his childhood.

"You were a boy then, Yule. You must weigh at least three stone more now than then. That vine—which looks quite dead if you ask me—is going to drop you on your arse." Tom looked ready to fight him to keep him from climbing up to the window on the second floor.

"I'll be fine." He grasped the vine, stuck the toe of his shoe into a crevice in the brick and pulled himself up. "Some things you don't forget how to do, no matter how long it's been."

"Is that Penelope's room?" Tom held his arms out to each side, as though he'd try to catch Yule should he slip or the vine give way.

Yule shook his head. "Victor's. We used to sneak out at night and go for long rambles. Or I'd come over and climb up so we could play late into the night." He grasped another vine directly above him, found another toehold, and raised himself another half foot. "Penelope's room is down at the end of the house. Her room faces north and no ivy would ever grow on it."

"What if the window's locked?"

Hanging ten feet off the ground, Yule stopped. "You would think of that, wouldn't you?" He sighed. "I guess I'll just have to break a pane. So you be ready with a diversion in case they hear me."

"A diversion?" Tom looked up at him, incredulous. "What kind of diversion?"

"For God's sake, Tom. I don't know. Go back inside and demand they give you breakfast or something." Yule pulled himself up another half-foot, so his head was now even with the bottom of Victor's window. His arms were beginning to tire. This had been much easier at the age of fifteen. "Tell them I went off in the carriage and abandoned you. I don't know. Use your imagination."

"You're not making this very easy for me, are you?"

Yule glanced down at his cousin's sullen face. "Please re-member this was all your doing. Had you kept your mouth shut…" Yule managed to hoist himself up and perch on a clump of the vine branches. He reached for the window sash, said a prayer, and pushed up. The wood gave some resistance, but finally slid upward. "Thank God!"

"Hooray!" Tom shouted from below.

"Be quiet for the love of God." Yule sent a vehement whisper to his cousin. He slid one long leg over the sill, pulled himself in and turned to Tom once more. "Go move the carriage down to the end of the driveway. I'll join you when I'm through."

"And how long with that be?" Tom's raised eyebrow said he didn't think all Yule had in mind was talking to Penelope.

"As long as it takes." The thought of speaking to Penelope in her bedroom, after several days of enforced celibacy, had Yule hoping their reconciliation would include more than a simple kiss to make up the quarrel.

First things first, however. He waved to Tom, shut the window, and crept to the door. Victor's room was directly across from the main staircase, so he had to be very quiet once he opened the door. Any untoward sound might bring someone to investigate. Slowly, he cracked the door open, praying it wouldn't squeak. The previous tenants must have used the room often, for the door opened easily, as though it had just been oiled. With a sigh of relief that one hurtle was past, Yule listened for a moment, then stuck his head out into the corridor.

Nothing stirred. He eased himself out of the room, taking the time to carefully close the door behind him. Then step by step, he slipped down the hallway, staying on the thick carpet in the center of the corridor. Only a few more steps until he reached the door to Penelope's room.

A burst of chatter from downstairs stopped him cold, sweat popping out on his forehead as he waited to see if anyone was coming up the stairs. Long moments later, when no one appeared, Yule released the breath he'd been holding and took the final step to stand before Penelope's bedroom door. He raised his hand to knock, then stopped. Even the noise of a quiet knock might carry down the stairs. Better be bold at this point. Yule grasped the handle and pushed down and inward.

The feminine room, all pale pink and white, was quiet, save for the crackling of the fire. Quiet and empty. Yule peered around, at the bed, at the dressing table, but Penelope was nowhere to be seen. After all his trouble, she wasn't even here. "Well, damn."

At his words, a very feminine shriek erupted from a spot on the other side of the bed in front of the fire. Then Penelope's head emerged over top of the mattress, eyes wide with shock. "Yule!"

His whole body relaxed at the sight of her, although one part of him began to tense again.

"What are you doing here?" She rose behind the bed, a delectable sight in an enticing white nightgown that hinted at the delights it hid. "How did you get in here?"

"I climbed up the ivy and came in through Victor's old room."

"You did what?" The incredulity on her face made him want to laugh, but he doubted that would endear him to her very much.

"I needed to talk to you, my love, and you wouldn't see me." He shrugged. "So I took matters into my own hands. Penelope, there are things you don't understand."

"I understand more than you wish I did." She turned her back on him. "I told you I didn't want to speak to you."

"Then don't speak. Just listen." Yule eased around the bed until he stood directly behind her. Her shoulders were trembling, as though she was trying to hold back tears. "I do not know exactly what Tom said to you, but—"

"He told me about that wretched wager you made with your grandfather." Her voice sounded choked. "That's more than you ever told me."

Alex certainly had been correct in saying everyone should tell their prospective brides about the wager immediately. He bitterly regretted that he'd ignored that advice. "I know, and I apologize sincerely from the bottom of my heart that my neglect to do so has caused you so much pain, my love."

"Don't call me that." The words came out a sob. "You don't mean it."

"I do mean it, sweetheart." Gently, he grasped her shoulders and turned her toward him. "Why do you doubt me?"

"Because you don't love me." Her tear-filled eyes accused him. "You only wanted to marry me to win that wager."

"Did Tom tell you that?" Yule didn't believe his cousin had been so deceptive and cruel, but he was at a loss to see how she would have come to the conclusion otherwise.

"No, not in those words. But he said you didn't have any idea who you were going to marry, and then you met me, and…and you didn't like me at all, Yule." She drew in a hitching breath. "You know you didn't. I tried everything I could think of to make you like me. To make you want to marry me, and you acted like you couldn't have cared less about me. Until suddenly, you did."

Well, that certainly was the truth of the matter. Except Penelope didn't know the reason behind his reluctance. When the sages said the truth shall set you free, they knew what they were talking about. "That is all true, my dear. But you don't understand the reason behind my stupid actions."

"The wager!" She gazed at him as though he was daft. "The wager with your grandfather and cousins that you were afraid I'd find out about."

"I wasn't afraid you'd find out." Yule frowned. "It didn't matter to me if you found out, although I did think if you knew, you'd tease me about it."

"You were afraid!" She raised her chin defiantly. "You agreed to a six month engagement, and then you suddenly wanted the wedding moved up. You wanted to marry me immediately but when that fell through, you settled for three weeks. Once I was down here in the country, I suppose there was less chance I'd find out until you married me."

Oh, Lord. "Penelope. Love, I can see the logic in what you say. I suppose it must have seemed like that to you, because you didn't have all the information. About the wager, and about me." He wanted to take her in his arms, but didn't think she'd stand for that, so he took her hands. "Yes, there is a wager between me, my grandfather and five of my cousins that we must all marry in order for us to win. We all have a year from this past August to marry. So I could very well have married you in June and done my part to win just the same."

Her brows knit themselves into a frown. "But you'd have had to keep the secret too long. That's why you insisted on marrying me now instead of later."

"I wanted to marry you immediately, my love, for the basest of reasons. Because I love you dearly and didn't want to have to wait six months to make love to you." Although that might have seemed obvious to him, apparently it had not been so obvious to Penelope.

Her eyes widened and her mouth dropped open. "But you didn't even like me when we met at the Kastners' house party."

"And this is where my stupidity comes into play. When I first saw you across the ballroom at the Kastners', I was flabbergasted by you. I thought you were the most beautiful young lady I'd ever seen, and when you came right up to me, I thought it was a dream come true." Had he followed his first instincts that night, how much easier might their path to happiness have been? "Then you called me by that awful, silly name and all I could see was the scrawny little seven-year-old girl I used to know."

Penelope gasped and her cheeks turned red. "Charlotte told me I was a ninny to have called you that."

"So, I was blinded to the fact you'd grown up into a very desirable young lady, fought against any attraction I had to you, until Christmas morning when my cousins made me see that I did have feelings for you." He squeezed her hands. "That I do love you, Penelope. God, how much I can't even tell you."

"You do?" She looked up at him, a pleading look in her eyes.

"How can you doubt it, sweetheart?" At last he gathered her to his chest. "I have thought about nothing but you ever since you made me see you as the perfect wife for me." What could he say to make her understand how absolutely mad he was about her? "I look at you now and cannot understand how I was such a blind fool. You are part of me, have been a part of me ever since we were children. That's why I never thought about marrying until the wager happened, why I never knew what I wanted in a wife. Because deep down I knew it was you." He smiled and kissed the top of her head. "When I first saw you at Kastner's, I thought 'There she is. She's what I want.'" Yule chuckled. "Until you called me that awful nickname."

"I am sorry about that my love." She snuggled against him. "I will never, ever call you Sissy again." She pulled away to look up at him sheepishly. "Except for that. That was the *very* last time, Yule."

"It's alright, sweetheart." He pulled her back to him, loving the way she felt pressed against his heart. "I don't mind so much anymore."

She relaxed into him, as if she'd suddenly had a weight lifted from her. "So you *do* love me?"

"With all my heart and body and soul." Yule pulled back until he could peer into her face. "Are you still going to marry me?"

"Oh, yes. Yes, I am." She threw her arms around him. "And the sooner the better. I've been so wretched these past few days without you."

"I have too, sweetheart." He kissed her hair, the scent of jasmine that clung to it intoxicating. His cock, deprived of her warmth for much too long, surged upward. Yule bit back a groan at what he was about to propose. "Would you like to make up for the days we've been apart?"

"What do you mean?"

He scooped her up in his arms, smothering her screech by pressing her face into his chest. He laid her on the frilly pink and white covers and quickly went and locked the door. When he turned back to her, his gaze intent on her, she sat up in the bed, pulling the covers around her.

"Yule! You don't mean to...It's not decent. We're in my father's house!"

He disregarded her outrage as he stalked back to the bed. "That only means we'll have to be very quiet, love."

She gazed at him, a sudden hunger in her eyes as she reached out to him.

He held up a finger, then headed to the far side of the bed and picked up the little doll from the floor where he'd spied it earlier. "I see Mrs. Phillpotts has continued to be company for you." The odor of freshly scorched linen wafted up to his nose and he raised an eyebrow at Penelope, who looked away. "She seems to have had a rough day already." He set the doll on Penelope's dressing table facing the wall. "Poor lady. Let's make certain she doesn't have another shock today."

Penelope giggled as Yule doffed his coat and slid onto the bed. "I dare not undress further, so we shall do things a little differently this time."

"We always do," she whispered, running her hand over his chest.

"I'm going to lie back, like this." He shifted so his head was on the pillow and he lay looking up at her. "And I'm going to unbutton my trousers, like this." Swiftly he loosed them, then opened the slit in his drawers. His cock sprang forward eagerly. "Now if you'll just raise your nightgown and climb on top of me…"

With one glance toward the door, Penelope lifted her gown, positioned herself carefully over him. Yule helped guide his member until he entered her, then slowly she slid down him, impaling herself inch by inch until he was fully seated inside her.

Penelope's face lit up with wonder. The sensation must be as incredible for her as it was for him. Oh, but he wished they could make noise. "Now rise up over me, then come back down, sweetheart. Like you're riding a horse."

"Riding a stallion, you mean." Smiling broadly, she rose up and slid down, the most exquisite sensation.

"That's right. Oh, yes." He thrust upward as she came down, reaching deeper into her tightness than he'd done before. Yule groaned, trying to keep his voice down, but wanting to moan with the ecstasy of possessing Penelope once more. With a finger, he stroked her nub, making her gasp and close her eyes, her face transfixed with passion. A guttural growl emerged from her lips, and she ground her hips against him.

As her tight sheath began to grasp him, she threw her head back, and he feared she was going to shriek, as much as he wanted to as he erupted deep inside her. They both shuddered, moaning low, as they reached the pinnacle together.

Panting deeply, Penelope collapsed onto his chest. Yule wrapped his arms around her, too spent to move any more. Slowly, they relaxed into one another, Penelope pillowing her cheek on his shoulder. "Can we stay just like this forever?"

"I suspect you will be summoned at some point, my love. And I doubt your parents will be pleased to discover me in your bed." He chuckled and ran his hand along her arm. "Although I believe they will be happy at our reconciliation."

"How will we tell them we've reconciled when you haven't been able to see me?" She rose up and looked him in the eyes. "Won't they be suspicious?"

"That depends."

"On what?"

"On whether or not they remember I used to scale the wall to visit Victor."

HALF AN HOUR later, picking her way gingerly downstairs—her secret tryst with Yule in her bed had left her much more sore than usual—Penelope hoped she'd been able to repair her appearance so that Mama and Papa wouldn't suspect what they'd been up to. It hadn't been easy without calling in her maid, but no one could know of Yule's presence in her bedchamber, so she'd had to manage by herself. Putting on her best smile, she entered the family drawing room.

"Penelope, my dear." Mama jumped up from where she'd

been pouring tea for her father and Charlotte. "I'm so pleased you've decided to join us." Her mother glanced at her father and whispered fiercely, "James, say something."

"You're looking very well, my dear." Dear Papa. That was his standard compliment, no matter the situation. Her face could be blotched with tears and he'd still say she looked very well.

"Thank you, Papa. I am feeling better, so I thought I should join you." Penelope sat carefully on the sofa and accepted a cup of tea.

"Have you thought any more about Yule, my dear?" Mama asked as delicately as she could. "He truly does love you, you know. He was quite inconsolable when you turned him away."

Penelope sipped her tea, trying to look as though she was thinking that statement over. "I have given it quite a bit of thought, Mama. And perhaps I was over hasty in judging Yule. At the very least, I feel now that I need to give him a chance to explain himself and that awful wager."

"Thank goodness, Penelope." Charlotte's face lit up. "I hated having to tell him to go away."

Mama's sigh of relief was rather loud, but truly heartfelt "I think that is very sensible of you, Penelope. I did think your dismissing Yule out of hand was childish. You are a young lady now, and need to act with more maturity." She turned to Papa, putting an insistent hand on his. "James, can you send a footman with a note to Welwyn Manor this instant asking Yule to return? I am certain he will wish to know of Penelope's change of heart."

"Very sensible, my dear." Papa gave her hand a pat, a smile touching his lips. "Let me ring for Stokes."

Before Papa could rise, as if already summoned, Stokes opened the door to the drawing room. "Mr. Ulysses Quarter-main."

Penelope sat up very straight, trying to look surprised.

Yule walked in, his countenance grave as he nodded to her parents. "Mr. and Mrs. St. Claire, Charlotte..." His gaze went to Penelope and his brows shot up. "...and Penelope. I am more than happy to see you are here."

"How fortuitous you have returned, Yule." Mama beamed at him and patted the spot beside her. "Please have a seat. Mr. St. Claire was just about to send you a note asking you to return, as Penelope has had a change of heart. Haven't you, my dear?"

"Yes, Mama." Penelope glanced at Yule, then cast her gaze down demurely. "I do believe I was wrong not to give you a chance to explain the circumstances of this wager."

"Thank goodness, Penelope." Yule sat beside Mama, smiling broadly. "I had almost arrived home and suddenly thought, 'I must make one more try to see her.' I'm so glad I did."

"We are so very glad also, Yule." Mama patted his arm. "We were beginning to fear—" Mama frowned and drew her hand away. "What is this?" She held up a tiny piece of a greyish-looking stick.

Penelope gasped and Yule paled.

Papa leaned over to inspect the object. "I'd say that was a piece of the vine that covers the back wall of the house, my dear." He turned a bland gaze on Yule. "Doesn't it look like that to you, Ulysses?"

Yule opened his mouth, but no sound emerged.

Mama looked from Penelope's red face to Yule's white one. "Do you mean to tell me you climbed up the wall and…and entered the house without our knowledge…"

Penelope had to turn away from Mama's painful scrutiny before the heat in her cheeks gave away the truth of the matter.

"Penelope!"

She jumped at the harsh tone of Mama's voice. Oh, but this was not how she and Yule had planned for this meeting to go.

"Did he visit your bedchamber?" The sharp whisper conveyed all the horror of her mother's question.

"Whether I did or not is totally irrelevant, Mrs. St. Claire." Yule spoke up before Penelope could open her mouth to deny it. "As Penelope and I are getting married."

Penelope glanced from one parent to the other, not liking the storm she saw brewing in their faces. "That is correct, Mama, Papa. The wedding is less than a week away."

"If you insist, I could try to get a special license so we can be married immediately, but the Archbishop of Canterbury has been ill—so I've heard." Yule seemed to have pulled himself back from the brink of disaster, his voice firm and authoritative. "But why don't we simply continue on with the wedding plans for next week." He looked at Mama and smiled. "That way no eyebrows will be raised over a hasty marriage."

"Very well." Mama folded her hands in her lap. "We will continue with the wedding plans for next week. However—" She turned to Papa. "I believe it is time to remove the ivy from the rear wall." She peered at Yule, her lips pursed. "High time."

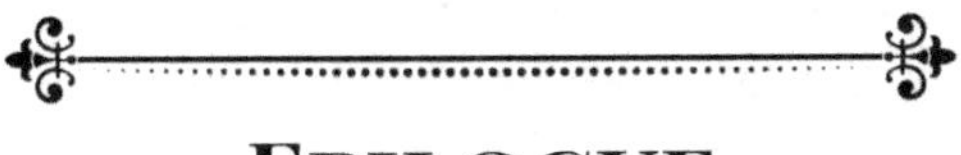

EPILOGUE

June 16, 1861
Mulberry Park, Hertfordshire

BRILLANT SUNSHINE DRENCHED the formal garden at the rear of the neat manor house where Yule and Penelope had been living together ever since their wedding in late January. The rocky start to their marriage notwithstanding, Yule could truthfully say his life had been idyllic ever since Christmas. As he and Penelope walked along the now very familiar paths of the garden, the word *idyllic* reverberated in his head. For someone who hadn't any idea of who to marry when the wager had first been proposed, he had to admit he had already gained far more than he'd ever realize if and when the larger wager was won.

"You're not tiring yourself out are you, my dear?" Yule couldn't help worrying about his little siren, walking sedately on his arm.

"I am fine, Yule. You really must stop badgering me." Penelope's long-suffering sigh was aimed squarely at him. "Walking in the garden is good for me. And I love seeing all the beautiful blooms. It quite changes every few days and I must see everything new."

"But you have insisted on walking in the heat of the day, love. I don't want you swooning.".

"I promise I have eaten luncheon—you dined with me, if you remember. So there is no reason I should be lightheaded. Oh, look." Penelope loosed his arm and ran toward a bed of hyacinths. "They are so pretty and the scent is beyond lovely." She bent to smell the plants, causing Yule to grab her from behind.

"Do not topple into the flowers, Penelope."

"I didn't plan on it." She grinned up at him, picked a blue bloom, then straightened and shoved it under his nose. "Doesn't it smell divine?"

He sniffed loudly. "It smells sweet."

"Men." She giggled and tucked the flower into the bodice of her deep blue gown. "You have no romantic sensibilities."

"I am the soul of romance, my love." He secured her arm again, determined to hang onto her this time. "You simply refuse to see it."

"Ha." She pursed her lips, tempting him to try and kiss her, but she continued too quickly for him to take that advantage. "I'd wager you don't know what today is."

"You'd lose that wager, my sweet." He laughed, happy to have won the innocent wager. "It is July 16th. I know because I wrote a letter this morning and consulted the calendar to be certain of the date."

"But what significance would that date have had?" Her beautiful face was alight with some secret.

"What significance *would* it have had?" He frowned, trying to figure out what she was hinting at. "I have no idea, love."

Penelope turned to face him, a knowing smile on her lips. "Today was supposed to have been our wedding day, silly."

"Oh, well, then no. I'm sure I did not remember that, if I ever knew it, sweetheart." Yule chuckled. "It was such a fleeting thought, wasn't it?"

She giggled. "Yes. I believe Mama and I hit upon it and not five minutes later, you were advocating for an immediate wedding."

"And a good thing too, in the end." Yule ran his hand over

Penelope's exceedingly large belly. "We'd never have made it till today to marry."

"As it is, we scarcely got married in time for this to be termed an 'early' baby with no one the wiser." She put her hand over his. "Do you think Mama and Papa know we anticipated our wedding night—by over a month?"

"I will be supremely happy to think they didn't know we anticipated it in their own house." Yule still couldn't quite believe he'd been that bold. There would have been hell to pay several times over had they been caught.

"One can be thankful for stoutly built houses. Oh!" Penelope put her hand to her belly, a pained expression on her face.

"What's wrong, love?" Yule was instantly on alert. He wouldn't be able to truly rest until the baby arrived and he knew both mother and babe were safe. With still more than three months to go, he was going to be very weary by September.

"Your son just gave me a great kick in my side." Smiling, she rubbed the offended area.

"Or daughter." Yule was always quick to point out the child might not be a boy. "Girls can be just as rambunctious as boys." He kissed her mouth and took her arm again. "You were proof of that."

"I suppose I was, although you must admit, I have changed my ways."

Yule snorted as he turned them back toward the house. "I would not vouch for that myself, my dear. You are just as boisterous now as you have ever been. Which is why I have to keep an eye on you and Rowena."

"You will not name our daughter Rowena." Penelope grimaced. "Or I promise to name our first son Marmaduke."

"I see nothing wrong with Marmaduke. One of Tom's younger brothers is named that. Perfectly respectable name." Yule could scarcely keep a straight face as he said it.

"Oh, you are lying, my love." Penelope gave a tinkling little laugh. "Although I could almost believe it. You have no sense at all with naming anyone."

"What do you mean?"

"Mrs. Phillpotts."

"Oh." He looked askance at her. "You don't like that name?"

"It was hardly a name a little girl would have chosen for her bosom companion." Penelope shook her head. "Where did you come up with it?"

"I'd heard Mother talk of a Mrs. Phillpotts, a friend of hers from home I believe. I thought it sounded grown up, like a person who would watch over you." Yule had never given a thought to the name before. It had somehow just come to him as he gave the doll to Penelope.

"And she did." Penelope laid her head on his shoulder. "Until you returned to watch over me instead." She glanced up at him. "Is that why you suggested I leave her in my bedroom at home when we married? Because her job to watch over me was done?"

Yule shook his head, looking sheepish. "No, not exactly. I just thought it best to leave her at your home so she wouldn't have to spend the rest of her days with her head turned to the wall."

The End

About the Author

Jenna Jaxon is a best-selling author of historical romance, writing in a variety of time periods because she believes that passion is timeless. She has been reading and writing historical romance since she was a teenager. A romantic herself, Jenna has always loved a dark side to the genre, a twist, suspense, a surprise. She tries to incorporate all these elements into her own stories.

She lives in Virginia with her family and a small menagerie of pets—including two vocal cats, one almost silent cat, two curious bunnies, and a Shar-pei mix named Frenchie.

Blog: www.jennajaxon.wordpress.com
Facebook: facebook.com/jenna.jaxon
Twitter: @Jenna_Jaxon
Instagram: passionistimeless
TikTok: @jennajaxon1